CASE STUDIES IN
MARKETING

Dr. Suresh Abhyankar
B.Sc., PGDM (FAM), MPM, Ph.D

VISHWAKARMA
PUBLICATIONS VP ™

Case Studies in Marketing

First Edition - October 2015
© Author

ISBN 978-93-83572-65-6

Published by:
Vishwakarma Publications
283, Budhawar Peth, Near City Post,
Pune- 411 002.
Phone No: (020) 20261157
Email: info@vpindia.co.in
Website: www.vpindia.co.in

Cover Design
Abhishek Darekar - Vishwakarma Publications

Typeset and Layout
Goldfish Graphics, Pune.

Foreword

Many management institutes use the case study method for explaining the intricacies of decision making in Marketing Management. Most of the cases are based on strategic decision making, which is not required by the fresh MBAs coming out of most of the institutes, barring the IIMs. All MBAs are required to spend their initial years at much lower levels, where strategic decision making is not involved. These students do not have proper exposure to the industrial atmosphere and also have very basic knowledge levels. Most of the students do not even undertake the compulsory six-week project work and submit old reports, sometimes without even changing the names. Obtaining company certificates has become child's play with easy software and no check on authenticity. Thus, students do not understand a thing when they actually start working in Marketing.

Also, while they expect that they shall be taking strategic decisions, they find instead that they are required to work at the basic level and get frustrated. This book will give them an insight into ground level realities. This book looks at the decisions that are required to be taken at the Area Manager (ASM) / Branch Manager (BM) levels and try to give them an insight into ground level problems.

As in Management, particularly Marketing Management, there are no 'ONE RIGHT ANSWER' situations. I have not given solutions to any of the cases, but I expect these cases to be discussed and various right answers to be sought for them. In case any faculty feels that I should personally give my answer, I may give them in person (if invited) or by e-mail. I look forward to receiving queries on the cases.

Dr. Suresh Abhyankar
drsureshabhyankar@gmail.com
+91 9822 06 7088
www.sellingskillspune.com

Table of Contents

C H A P T E R   1

Cases in
Sales Management

Case Study - 1

AGARWAL DISTRIBUTORS

Bipin Agarwal was trying to acquire the distribution of a large MNC for the Pimpri- Chinchwad area. The company sales officer had given him the following facts:

1. Turnover was 4 Crores per month.
2. The margin was 5%.
3. A distributor should always have 15 days paid stock with him.
4. Market outstanding was expected to be 15 days sales.
5. The company would clear all claims within 15 days after the credit note was issued.
6. Claims were, on an average, equal to one week's sales volume.

7. Distribution expenses were around 2% of the turnover.

When Bipin enquired about the previous distributor, the company sales officer said that his distribution was unsatisfactory and so the turnover was low. Bipin asked him to give details of where the distributor was found to be wanting in his services. The sales officer gave him the following details:

1. Not all the retailers were getting service from the distributor.
2. His visits were infrequent and not regular.
3. Orders booked were not being supplied the next day, but were supplied whenever the distributor sent deliveries of other companies.
4. He was not giving replacements of expired goods and consumer complaint goods.
5. He was not extending credit to most of the retailers.
6. He was dependent on wholesalers rather than retailers.

The retailers said that the previous distributor was not extending credit in the market and so the sales were low. Actually, the product had a good potential and consumer demand. Bipin asked a few retailers as to what their purchase volumes at a time were. Most of the retailers gave a figure that was low but they still expected credit and higher frequency of service. Bipin then asked them if they were getting replacements. Most of the retailers said the replacements were okay earlier, but later the distributor stopped them saying that the company representative was not issuing credit notes, so he had stopped replacing goods.

The previous distributor said that the company had a dumping policy. The investments in stock and market outstanding was more than 60 days, the credit notes for damaged stocks and replacements were not done every month, as they were signed by the Area Manager who came once every three months. The company took signed cheques and was supposed to deposit them eight days after the distributor received the stocks, but many times, the cheque came to the bank first and the stocks were received later. So, he was not earning anything from the business, and many times, faced losses. He said it was only after he went to the local Distributors Association, that the company cleared all dues and issued credit notes. He was having some stock that needed to be transferred to a new distributor and he would give the NOC for the appointment of a new distributor, only after the remaining stock was lifted and he was paid for the same.

Questions

1. What should Bipin do? Should he accept the business or not? Give reasons.

2. Under what conditions should Bipin accept the business readily? The margins cannot be increased.

Suggested Answer

Bipin should not accept the dealership in the current situation as,

1. His investment is nearly 1.5 months i.e. 3% per month will be reduced from his margin.

2. Distribution expenditure of 2% takes the total expenditure to 5% i.e. the total margin offered.

Case Study - 2

ASHOK APTE'S DILEMMA

Ashok Apte, Area Sales Manager, SKACO Ltd., was drowned in deep thought. He was thinking about the problem at hand. This was the first time that he was facing a situation where he had to take a decision, but was not sure what the right course of action would be and what decision he should take.

He had come for his monthly meeting to his regional office the day before at Bandra, Mumbai. During the lunch break, Narayan, the Sales Administrative Manager had taken him aside and said, "I want to tell you something about your subordinate. I have not mentioned this to anyone as yet; but I thought I should discuss the matter with you before I speak to the boss (the Regional Manager)." Narayan then told him about his recent visit to Goa for the warehouse audit of the Goa agent and how the Sales Manager of the Goa agent, Mr. Pandurang had reported to him that Ramesh Talolikar, the sales officer in-charge of Goa had come for his market visit accompanied by his newly- wedded wife. Narayan said, "Ashok, you must take appropriate action before something goes wrong." Knowing Narayan's behavior, Ashok knew that he must have already informed the Regional Manager (RM) about it and the RM must have asked him to let Ashok handle it. Since Ashok was a star Area Sales Manager (ASM) and had reported good sales for the previous month, at least in the morning session the RM would not take up such matters with him unless it affected the sales of his area. As expected by Ashok, the RM did not refer to the matter during the meeting, or even during drinks and dinner during the evening.

Background – A Flashback

Ashok was preparing his report of the previous month and the plan for the next month, but his mind was more on what action should be taken on Ramesh. He first started thinking about Ramesh, who was a tall, fair and handsome fellow. Ramesh had joined SKACO after a stint with VST (Vazir Sultan Tobacco Ltd.) and was given a posting in Mumbai city. After working under Mr. Arvind in Mumbai, Ramesh requested the RM for a transfer to the Rest of Maharashtra and Goa area under Ashok who was the ASM. The reason he cited was that he would like to get up country work experience and his interest was in handling the distributors on his own. While privately talking to Ashok, Ramesh had said, "Arvind troubles me a lot, because he is jealous of my personality as he is a short fellow with ordinary looks." Ashok was also a tall handsome person with an attractive personality and so Ramesh felt that his problem would be solved.

Ashok found Ramesh to be a good worker and very ambitious too. Ramesh had enrolled himself for a part-time diploma course in marketing from Mumbai University and had plans for upward mobility as soon as possible. He was found to be good at reporting and achieved his targets every month. He was also found to be enthusiastic in the development of his area and came out with novel proposals for sales promotions. Ramesh was an asset to Ashok's team. He had many offers from various other organizations that he did not consider. He used to say, "I am getting good guidance under Ashok and am learning a lot many things here. I will only accept an offer that will give me vertical promotion and high responsibility; I will never go for horizontal shifting."

Any action that is severe can lead to loss of a good team member. The offence does not always require severe punishment but needs to be taken cognizance of.

Ashok started thinking of previous examples of such types and he could remember only incidences where sales officers had done false reporting of tours, when they had actually not gone on tour at all. In all such incidences, sales officers were punished and many of them lost their jobs for these reasons. Ashok himself, as a sales officer, had taken his wife with him on a tour of Nasik and Pune with the permission of his RM. Actually, Ashok had applied for leave on a Monday as he wanted to take his wife to Pune for some religious function after working in Mumbai on Saturday. Due to urgent work, his RM sent him to Nasik on Saturday and Pune on Monday and permitted him to take his wife along for the tour, as the work at both Nasik and Pune was of a short duration. The RM even allowed Ashok to hire a taxi for the entire tour. He had said, "This work can be done by you and you alone and so, do the work and enjoy the trip with your wife!"

The Company

SKACO Ltd. was a subsidiary of a multinational corporation dealing in FMCG products. It had three manufacturing units in India, strategically located in Faridabad near Delhi, catering to the North and the West; at Howrah near Kolkata, catering to the eastern parts of India along with Odisha, Bihar and Jharkhand; and one at Bangalore, catering to entire South India. The company operated with four regional offices headed by Regional Managers (RMs) at Delhi for North, Mumbai for West, Kolkata for East and Chennai for South. Regional Managers at all these four places reported to the General Sales Manager (GSM) who sat at the head office in Delhi. Every state was headed by an ASM, except for Maharashtra (where Mumbai city and the rest of Maharashtra had separate ASMs); Kolkata, (where Kolkata city and the rest of West Bengal had separate ASMs); and Chennai, (where Chennai city and the rest of Tamilnadu had separate ASMs). The ASM of the Rest of Maharashtra had the additional charge of Goa and the ASM of Rest of West Bengal had the additional charge of Sikkim and Bhutan. All the ASMs had 4 - 8 sales officers reporting to them.

SKACO Ltd. gave daily allowances of four types to all their Sales Officers (SO):

1. Headquarter (HQ) allowance when SO worked at his HQ.
2. Full day allowance when SO went out of HQ and returned in the evening/night.
3. Night-away allowance when SO went out of his HQ and stayed out.
4. Night-away actual allowance when SO travelled out of HQ and charged actual expenses up to a prescribed limit.

SKACO Ltd. was one of the top five companies in the sector and was known for good remunerations. Since its products were well-accepted, pushing sales was not very difficult. However, they still needed a constant push and alertness about the prevalent competition.

The Dilemma

Ashok had various options for taking action against Ramesh. Serious action was due if

1. Ramesh had not worked for the market and had falsely reported about market work.

2. Ramesh had charged the travel, lodging and boarding cost of his wife to the company.

Ashok called the accountant and asked him for Ramesh's travelling expense statement for his Goa tour. On inspecting it he found that Ramesh had claimed only his own travelling expenditure and he had charged upcountry night-away daily allowance, instead of actual hotel expenses. Ramesh went to Goa from Mumbai and returned to Mumbai directly. He left on Saturday night and returned on Monday morning, but charged allowances only from Monday to Saturday. So no financial offence was done.

Ashok next contacted Pandurang in Goa and enquired whether Ramesh worked for the market properly. Pandurang said that every day Ramesh reported at the right time at the distributor point and worked full-time. While working in Panaji he went to his room for lunch and at Madgaon, Ramesh stayed back after work and came to Panaji late as he called his wife to meet him in Madgaon in the afternoon. So there was no problem on the work front also.

The only problem that was left was taking his wife on tour without the knowledge of the ASM, and the ASM felt that this should not become a precedent for more of such incidences.

Ashok could not let go off the incident and also could not let Ramesh go scot-free. Some action needed to be taken that would become a deterrent to others so that no one else would do so again.

Questions

What action do you suggest against Ramesh? Why?

Case Study - 3

PICKWICK BECOMES PROFITABLE

When Kanchan Ambekar approached this author in his capacity as a marketing consultant in Bangalore, asking him to join his organization Primlaks Waffles Pvt. Ltd., of which he was the CEO, the company was going through a very bad phase. Kanchan had taken the posting as a challenge. For understanding the situation, we must look into the history of the company.

Primlaks Waffles Pvt. Ltd., was a company started by an NRI group. They launched the Pick Wick brand with much fanfare in 1982. The marketing team had joined from a reputed biscuit-making company. After spending a lot of money and enough time, the owners felt that the brand was not doing well in spite of heavy expenditure on marketing. The company decided to curtail the expenditure and concentrate only on Maharashtra and Gujarat where they had steady volumes. So from 1986, they curtailed expenditure on the sales force and marketing. The sales went down and the company started losing money. When in 1992, Kanchan, with experience in manufacturing in Rawalgaon joined the company, he found that there was no problem in the product and all that was missing was marketing expertise. He brought in a sales manager from his earlier company. They were able to stop the decline but could not bring the sales up.

During his visit to Bangalore, Kanchan met the author by chance at a local distributor point. Kanchan was quite impressed by his knowledge and working style. He came back to Bangalore again in the next month, this time with an offer. He asked Suresh to name the price and the designation he wanted to join Primlaks Waffles. Suresh asked for DOUBLE his current salary and wanted the designation of General Manager-Sales and Marketing. He would report directly to the CEO. In addition, he asked for a car without any upper limit on petrol consumption. His demands were fulfilled.

After coming to Pune, Suresh found that

1. The company had accumulated losses to the tune of Rs.1.5 Crores.

2. The company products were available in Maharashtra and Gujarat through their subsidiary company, Target Marketing Pvt. Ltd. (TMPL) as selling agent, and in metro cities Kolkata, Chennai and Delhi through super distributors only.

3. The factory worked for eight hours a day.

4. The sale was 1200 cartons, worth Rs.12 lakh per month.

5. Prices were not standardized and the distributors in Delhi, Chennai and Kolkata gave orders only when contacted and requested by Kanchan and that too, after getting extra discounts. Kanchan felt obliged to ensure payments to suppliers.

6. There was no expenditure on Marketing.

7. There was no POP material available.

8. Old stock was a big problem.

9. Shelf life was accepted as six months only.

10. The company was unable to replace date-barred products from the market.

11. The sales force was untrained and had low productivity and motivation.

There were some positive points also.

1. The quality was accepted by consumers as the best in the category.

2. There were many loyal consumers who insisted on buying their brand only.

Suresh knew that he had to start by increasing sales volumes first. This seemed impossible through the existing set-up, so he went in for a multi-pronged strategy as follows-

a. Appointing more super distributors in all the states of India.

b. Training the existing sales staff to improve productivity.

c. Increasing awareness in the consumers about the products.

Since there was no budget for marketing, he persuaded the company to sanction a few thousand rupees to get stickers made. He designed and produced stickers that could be stuck on the lids of plastic jars which he gave as QPS (Quantity Purchase Scheme) on Rs.1 and Rs.2 packs. In the first month itself, he reopened the states of Madhya Pradesh, Uttar Pradesh and Rajasthan with new super distributors. He standardized the pricing and decided minimum purchase norms (one canter load) against advanced demand draft only. This ensured that the super distributors purchased limited stock and sold it before it crossed the expiry date and also reduced transit damages, as it went as a full load of a canter.

The next step was to start training of existing staff and for this purpose, he created and executed the training program himself.

Within four months, the company started operating 24 hours, and was present in all the states of India except Orissa. He changed some of the packaging to give the products display value.

The company started getting operating profits within 6 months and wiped out accumulated losses within 18 months.

All this was possible because of consumer acceptance of the brand as a quality brand and the simple rule of selling, viz-

MAKE THE PRODUCT AVAILABLE TO MAXIMUM NUMBER OF CONSUMERS AND MAKE THE CONSUMERS AWARE OF ITS PRESENCE.

This was accomplished only through reaching out to more number of consumers (by appointment of super distributors all over India), making them aware through simple POP material.

If the consumer is aware of the product and the quality is good, then expenditure on marketing is not necessary.

Questions

1. What strategies were applied by Suresh for increasing the sales volumes?
2. What was done to avoid damages and expired products?
3. What ensures sales of any product?

Case Study - 4

OODAK MINERAL WATER

Mr. Devendra Patil was a farmer with a huge lot of irrigated land. His sister Savita was married to a software engineer and was now staying in the Bay area of California. Savita had two sons and a daughter all aged between 5 to 8 years. Savita came for a holiday after many years and visited her brother, Devendra. When she came, she was carrying a stock of mineral water bottles and she and her children would drink only bottled water. The moment she landed in Devendra's house, she requested him to get hold of at least 3-4 dozen mineral water bottles for her family's use while they stayed here.

During her stay, Devendra understood the need and importance of mineral water bottles, as even the visiting professionals from the city to his village and nearby towns required them. He was amazed to see people paying Rs.12/- for a litre of drinking water. He had a well in his land that had water all the year round and he supplied water by tankers to many villages during the summer season and charged Rs.1000/- for a tanker load of 10000 litres, i.e. Rs.1/- per litre inclusive of transport charges. He decided to explore the possibility of setting up a mineral water plant. He appointed a marketing consultant for the same.

The marketing consultant said, "We must do a feasibility survey and decide the strategy for marketing the product. We must also think of a good name for the product that is easy to remember and relate. We must also find suppliers of bottles, labels and the plant and machinery. We will need to appoint sales staff and purchase/hire delivery vehicles. We will also look for the advertising media for the promotion of the product." Devendra said, "You do whatever is required, but I would like to have this factory set up as fast as possible."

Market Survey Results

The marketing consultant conducted a survey of the entire district for mineral water and had the following results-

I- Competitors: The following brands were available in the market:

1. Bisleri
2. Bailey
3. Kinley
4. OOzone

Out of these products, Bisleri, and Bailey were available only in 'A' class outlets and were being sold at Rs.15/- per litre. Kinley was available at most of the stores in small quantities and was being sold at Rs.15/- per litre. The maximum sale at all stores, restaurants and bars was that of OOzone that was manufactured in Pune district and was being retailed at Rs.12/- per litre.

II- Retail Margins: Bisleri, Bailey and Kinley were being sold to retailers at Rs.13/- per litre with a promotional offer of one litre free with every box of 12 one litre bottles, effectively giving a margin of Rs.4/- per bottle (nearly 23%). OOzone was being supplied to retailers at Rs.9/- per litre and had a promotional offer of two one litre bottles per box of 12 one litre bottles and one box free on the purchase of five boxes. As most of the retailers purchased five boxes every time, their effective margin was nearly 45%.

III- Investment: It was advised that a PET bottle manufacturing unit should also be started along with the water purifying and bottling plant; and so the total investment exclusive of the land was coming to Rs.15 Lakh.

IV- Production Cost: Production cost was expected to be Rs.2.5/- per litre at 50% utilization of capacity and was dropping to Rs.1.5/- per litre at full capacity utilization in one shift, inclusive of all taxes.

V- Selling Cost Inclusive of Transport: Cost of selling was the major expense. If two quality sales persons were appointed along with a van driver and a loader/delivery boy, the monthly cost was coming to Rs.2.5/- per litre at 50% capacity utilization and was dropping to Rs.1.5 at full capacity utilization in one shift.

VI- Pricing for OOdak: The marketing consultant suggested that for entering the market effectively, they must ensure that OOzone was out of market; so they must use the market penetration strategy and fix a price below OOzone. So the price was decided to be Rs.8/- per litre with the same promotional offer of two, one litre bottles per box of 12 one litre bottles and one box free on purchase of five boxes, making the effective margin 70%. Once OOzone was evicted out of the market (their transport cost was higher as they had to travel longer distance) the price could be increased slowly to Rs.9/- per litre.

VII- Frequency of Coverage: OOzone covered the market once a week with a large truck not covering all the outlets; so OOdak decide to cover the market twice a week with a tempo load reaching all the outlets more frequently, leading to less number of retailers buying five boxes of OOZone and saving on the promotional cost of OOdak.

VIII- Advertising Plan: They decided to do wall paintings in surrounding villages and towns and few road-side hoardings on the state highway that passed through these towns and villages.

They also decided to have full page newspaper advertisements in the local newspapers announcing the introduction of the product.

The OOdak launch was a great success and it captured 80% market share within four months.

Questions

1. What were the pre-introduction preparations for OOdak?

2. Why did the consultant insist on the survey? Was it necessary? What would happen if the survey was not done?

Case Study - 5

THE CASE OF POPICE - DISPOSABLE ICE CUBE BAGS

Popsicle Enterprises of Bangalore came out with a very innovative idea of disposable ice cube bags for people who needed ice cubes during parties being hosted at their homes.

Need Development: Normally all the refrigerators had two ice trays that gave 32 to 40 ice cubes of different sizes. For a house party of 3-4 couples, one needed to have all these cubes to serve one round of drinks.. The refrigerators took many hours for setting of the ice, so for a second round of drinks to be served or for cold drinking water, there was no ice left.

People used to ask their guests (if they were close friends) to bring in ice while coming for a party or bought ice from the local ice factory. The ice from the ice factory was not hygienically clean and good and it was only in an emergency that people used the ice from there.

Ice cubes from clean water were available in cities like Mumbai and Delhi only but not available readily in other cities. Purchasing more number of ice trays and using them on such occasions was not possible as the freezer had limited space.

Disposable ice cube bags were a better alternative.

Market: All cities in India with all middle class consumers having medium size refrigerators.

Distribution: The company planned to appoint distributors at all places that would distribute the products in all novelty and stationery shops.

Promotions: Since the product was low priced and margins were very slim, only quantity discounts were planned.

Fig. 1.1: Popice disposable ice cube bags packing

Price: The MRP was planned at Rs.18/- with a retail margin at 15%, distributor margin at 10% and quantity discount of additional 10%.

Market testing: The product was market-tested and was to be acceptable only if the customers were convinced about the product. No customers demanded the product as it was unknown to them and there was no awareness campaign for the same.

I had suggested house to house campaigning to create awareness, and then to go in for distribution to the company in my capacity as a marketing consultant. The cost of house to house campaigning with 10% productive calls and minimum 100000 (one lakh) calls was very high and the manufacturers were not prepared to spend so much.

Result: No distributor accepted the distribution of the product without the promise of marketing efforts from the company like advertisements or proper promotion to create awareness of the product.

The product had limited success in Bangalore only. The advent of ice cube machines and the ready availability of ice cubes killed the chances of success of the product.

Questions

1. Why was the product not successful?
2. What strategies could have made the product acceptable?

Case Study - 6

SNACKLES BISCUITS

Monita Foods Pvt. Ltd., a Mumbai-based company manufacturing ice-cream cones for various reputed organizations, and canapés that were sold in the confectionery market and to hotels and restaurants, decided to expand the business through the addition of new products in the similar sector and contacted the author as their marketing consultant. A survey of the biscuit market brought him the following results:

Current Players: There were many biscuit manufacturers who were vying for market share in-

- The glucose biscuit sector. Prominent amongst them were Parle Products, Britannia, Bakeman's, Maharaja, Samrat etc. Parle had over 80% market share, Britannia around 12% and the rest of the brands accounted for the remaining 8% in the urban markets. I In the price-sensitive rural areas local brands and duplicates of prominent brands (Paro, Panama etc.) were sold maximum with very little sale of prominent brands.

- Britannia was very strong in the Marie biscuit segment and ruled the market with almost 90%, with others accounting for the rest.

- In the cream biscuit segment, Britannia was again the market leader in most flavours but Parle had a lead in the chocolate flavour with their brand Bon-Bon. However, every town had its own locally-made cream biscuits that sold only because they were cheap.

- In the salted biscuits segment, Parle Monaco was the market leader with Britannia's "Sixer" being sold in small quantities. The salted biscuit segment had many gaps in terms of smaller packets, as Monaco had a bigger pack and Sixer was being sold loose. Salted biscuits had a lesser shelf life as they were more hygroscopic and became soft after the pack was opened.

- Cookies were being sold locally and the only player was Britannia with "Goodday" that was priced only for upper middle and higher class customers. The others settled for cookies being sold locally by bakeries.

Pricing: Both Parle and Britannia had franchises all over India, reducing their costs of manufacturing and transportation and both had a policy of blocking the entry of new players by selling their products at low margins, so that no new player was able to enter the biggest biscuit market, that of the GLUCOSE sector. The distributor and retail margins were also low, but since the volumes were very high and money rotation was fast, everyone was happy selling these products at low margins. Entry in this market was very difficult even with high margins being offered to distributors and retailers as this would lead to high MRP of the product, thus repelling the customers.

Distribution: All the biscuit marketers used VMS and had distributors all over India, so a distribution set up was to be created by Monita Foods by appointing a super distributor in Ahmedabad, Mumbai and Pune.

Scope for New Product: Only innovative new products had a scope for acceptance, like Britannia's 'Little Hearts' which was instantly accepted due to its novelty. The products had to be sold in a very attractive pack and could not be priced more than Rs.5/-.

Packaging: It was decided that the product should be sold in a strip of twelve pouches containing 50 grams of Snackles and twelve such strips to be packed in an outer container box.

The distributor would get the box for Rs. 500 and would sell every strip for Rs. 50, giving enough margins for both distributors and retailers.

Suresh suggested that the product should initially be contract-manufactured and once the product settled in the market, a manufacturing facility may be created. The owners decided to get the product contract manufactured and gave an order for the first lot to the contract manufacturer without taking a trial run of the machinery to be used by the contract-manufacturer. The contract manufacturer was a childhood friend of one of the directors and they had full faith in him.

The Sale:

The first lot was delivered by the contract manufacturer and was immediately dispatched to the super distributors, who in turn supplied it to the distributors and retailers. On the very first day of distribution, the distributors complained that many strips were empty and there were no biscuits and they wanted the entire stock to be taken back and fresh stock to be sent as replacement. The owners said, "Let us check the entire stock and find out the extent of empty pouches and send that much additional stock to the distributors."

The distributors reported that 80% of the stock was with empty pouches and as many as 50% empty pouches. These figures were refuted by the contract manufacturer and the owners of the company. The dispute prolonged and the distributors refused to pay unless the problem was solved. Suresh tried to mediate and asked the owners to send the replacement stock and resolve the matter. The Mumbai and Pune super distributors accepted the replacements and said that they did not want to continue. But in the case of the Ahmedabad super stockist, both parties refused and the matter went to the courts with the super distributor filing cases of cheating. The business stopped as all the parties involved lost faith in the manufacturer.

The cheating case took many years to come up for hearing and both the parties accepted out of court settlement.

Questions

1. What do we learn from the case?

2. "The trial of product manufacturing and packaging are very important before it is actually launched." Do you accept the statement after going through the case study?

3. What action would you have taken when the packaging complaints were received?

Case Study - 7

PUSH PROMOTIONS ON NAVIN KETCHUP

Chordia Food Products Ltd. (CFPL) manufacturers of Pravin and Navin brands of ketchup and Pravin brand of pickles headed by Mr. Pradeep Chordia, a GOLD medalist food technologist from the Institute of Food Technology, Mysore was famous for the quality standards of their pickles and ketchups. The products were being sold in Maharashtra, Gujarat, Karnataka, Tamilnadu and Rajasthan. The selling was done through the company sales staff and a VMS (Vertical Marketing System) of distributors and retailers. All the products were sold against advanced Demand Draft payment system.

Fig. 1.2: Pravin Pickles

The pickle market had various players in it like Bedekar, Kepra, Nilon, Mother's, MTR etc., along with Pravin & Navin (Jain Special), brands and local unbranded products that were being sold by retailers. Pickles were purchased by consumers in small packing and by institutional buyers (hotels & restaurants), in bulk packing of 5 & 10 kg. The institutional buyers are mostly not quality-conscious and purchase any pickle that is available at the lowest price, since they offer pickles to customers free of charge as accompaniment to their Rice Plate or other food preparations. So most branded pickle manufacturers concentrated more on the consumer sales. With so many players vying for limited market place, the pickles market is very competitive and the margins are very low. So CFPL had introduced Pravin and Navin ketchups in the market.

Fig. 1.3: Pravin & Navin Ketcups

The ketchup market is a very quality-conscious market and consumers purchase products that have brand recognition. The market is dominated by Kissan (HUL), Maggi (Nestle) with Kissan being the brand leader. Also, the market is divided into two parts - that of consumers buying branded ketchups and institutional buyers (hotels, restaurants and food stall holders), purchasing unbranded products that are available at cheap rates. The institutional buyers are catered to by local manufacturers who produce ketchups in small scale quantities at home on a daily basis as additional income for their households and are willing to sell at a low price for getting continuous business. Small scale industrial manufacturers also produce ketchups but they concentrate in selling it to mostly highway restaurants and B & C grade restaurants in cities and towns where this ketchup is mostly used for making instant tomato soup. This sector is also very price conscious and competitive in nature, so profit margins are very low.

CFPL with its high quality ingredients and high quality product concentrated on direct consumer market and because of the established pickles market, was able to get good distribution. The problem was that the retailers were not pushing the product enough to get high volume sales. CFPL appointed the author as their marketing consultant to improve their sales. Suresh first concentrated on the product distribution and for that he trained the sales staff in improving the sales distribution to increase STRs in the market and the width of distribution.

His second step was to train the distributors on product storage (pickles need to be stored in maximum five high stacks to avoid breakages in the lower stack) and use the FIFO strategy that helped reduction in damages and age bar stocks, which was reducing the distributor's margin (CFPL gave a fixed percentage of margin to take care of transit/storage damages). This improved the distributors' motivation in selling CFPL products.

The third step was to develop promotional strategies for CFPL products, since margins in pickles were very low and there was no scope for promotional expenses. Margins in ketchups were good and had scope for increasing the MRP also, as the difference between Pravin and Navin ketchups MRP and that of Kissan and Maggi was very high. The gap between Kissan and Maggi's market share with Pravin and Navin was also very high and a small percentage of market shares could also give very high volume gains for Pravin and Navin sales without HUL or

Nestle ever understanding the drop in sales (their volumes were very high).

Pravin and Navin ketchups offered one bottle free on every carton of twelve bottles as normal continuous push promotion, so Suresh decided to develop a quantity purchase scheme only to create a good push for the product. He first increased the MRP by nearly 10% to Rs. 42/- for Pravin (Kissan MRP was Rs.60/-) and Rs.45/- for Navin and then came out with quantity discount scheme for Mumbai city as follows-

One box- one bottle free (normal scheme).

Two boxes—four bottles free.

Three boxes - seven bottles free.

Five boxes – one box (12 bottles) free.

The scheme period was for 45 days and any retailer who bought maximum quantity in any distributor area, was promised an additional box of ketchup free. The scheme was the same on both, Pravin and Navin ketchups and if a retailer purchased the quantity in mixed variety, the free bottles were of Pravin which was lower priced. The sales staff was motivated by declaring incentives for achieving targeted quantity in the given period. They were advised to motivate the retailers to sell the products at a lower price and attract more customers by putting up boards outside the shops, announcing the price comparison of ketchups.

The scheme was a great success and five times the normal volume sales was achieved during the scheme period. The sales settled at nearly a double level afterwards.

This also had the additional side-effect - Mr. Thiuambalam, the Country Head of Heinz called Suresh (both had worked together in Smithkline Beecham) to discuss the marketing strategies adopted by Navin ketchup (Navin was selling more quantity than Heinz) and CFPL was given the contract to manufacture Heinz at their Shirwal unit.

Questions

1. Do you think customers are brand-loyal for products like ketchup?

2. What strategy was used to attract customers towards Navin and Pravin ketchups?

Case Study - 8

TEEN 6 TEEN

Manasi Cosmetics was a firm started by a chemist who had many years experience of working in companies like Lakme and Tips & Toes and who was an expert in colour cosmetics with work experience in Gala of London. With such expertise, he wanted to come out with quality colour cosmetics that would readily be accepted by Indian consumers. I was called upon to be his marketing consultant. Initial introduction was planned for Maharashtra state- (which was a major market for branded colour cosmetics).

Market Research: Market research was planned in two parts and was conducted in Mumbai, Nasik, Aurangabad, Ahmednagar and Kolhapur markets. No consumer research was done -only the wholesalers, distributors and retailers were surveyed to get a fix on the market. Few manufacturers in Mumbai (making unbranded products) were also visited.

1) **Current Players:** The colour cosmetics market was totally dominated by Lakme with nearly 70-80% market share of branded goods. The remaining part was Tips & Toes, Gala of London & Max Factor, with Lakme being present all over Maharashtra, in the premium range and Elle18 at Rs.18/- as an economy range. Unbranded products were present all over Maharashtra through a network of wholesale dealers selling cheap products coming from Sadar Bazar of Delhi or Cutlery Market in Mumbai. These cheap products were manufactured by using used X-ray films, old cinema films and cheap colours. These cheap products were given labels with partly English

& partly Arabic prints, with fake bar codes to show that they were imported products. Cheap products had brand names like Mona, Tina, Evening of Paris etc. and these products had a limited shelf life of one or two months.

2) Current Market Condition: Only higher class and higher middle class customers were using branded cosmetics and all others bought the cheap products for occasional use. Colour cosmetics were found to have a seasonal sales pattern. The sales season started from Nagpanchami in the month of Shrawan and ended in Diwali (festival season) and the second season started in March and ended in May (marriage season). During seasonal sales, the cheap products sold the highest even in the rural markets.

Retailers were keen on selling the cheap products as the margins were very high; most of the cheap products were available at Rs.8-to 12 for a box of dozen bottles to the distributors and they sold them to retailers at Rs.50-60 a box of dozen bottles. Retailers sold these bottles for Rs.20-30 per unit making big profits, since the cheapest branded product was L18 at Rs.18/-. The consumers were willing to pay a little extra for what was supposed to be an imported product.

Production Plan & Pricing Decisions: The product name was decided as 'Teen 6 Teen' to relate the product to teenagers and the logo was designed by a professional artist. The original plan of setting up a manufacturing unit in the Mumbai suburbs was dropped and it was planned to start production at someone else's chemical manufacturing unit, till the market was set, as the financiers backing the project backed out at the last minute.

Since the distributors expected a minimum of 20% margin and retailers demanded 40% margin, the MRP (maximum retail price) was decided to be Rs.16/- as against the one earlier planned at Rs.12/-. This left the manufacturer very little margin for running additional promotions. The retailers wanted six months credit (equal to the shelf life of the product) initially and then they were willing to pay order to order (payment of previous bill when next supplies are given i.e. one bill to be kept pending always).

When Suresh discussed these matters with the manufacturer and the required minimum capital, they decided to introduce the product only in one city i.e. either in Pune or in Mumbai. In Mumbai, getting the product distributed would have required a high inventory and capital inputs, as the number of retailers selling colour cosmetics in Mumbai then were around 8000 to 9000 as against only 1200 retailers in Pune who sold colour cosmetics. So Pune was selected as a market for introduction.

Selection of Distributor: A distributor located in Shukrawar Peth which is closer to Tulsibaug and Mandai, which are the major areas selling colour cosmetics and Raviwar Peth i.e. a wholesale market in Pune was selected for better service to the high-selling areas.

Selection of Sales Team: Because of limited finances available, no sales person was appointed (fixed liability). Instead, the distributor was offered additional two percent margin towards sales staff expenses.

The Launch: The launch of the product was low-key and no newspaper advertisement or banners were put up (financial restraint) and the product was placed in major kangan (ladies specialty) stores in all parts of the city with display windows being booked for two months, getting high visibility. Major stores in Camp and Ferguson College Road were given demo kits for the girls to try the nail paint shades. Initially, nail paints (12 shades), lip sticks (12 shades) and eyeliner sticks were introduced. Overall 100 outlets in all parts of Pune city including the high selling areas of Mandai and Tulsibaug stocked the products.

Fig. 1.4: Teen 6 Teen Lipsticks with 30 Shades

Fig. 1.5: Complete Product Range of Teen 6 Teen

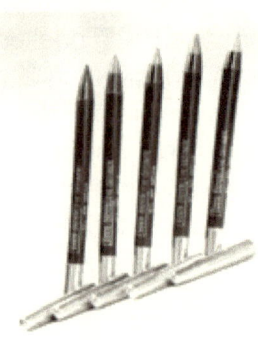

Fig.1.6: Teen 6 Teen Range of Eye Liners

Sales Pattern: The eyeliner sticks which were priced much lower than the market rates, were an instant success and also the nail paint removers sold very well as they were also priced lower than the other products (there was no competition). Some shades of nail paints which were unique sold instantly.

In addition to shop sales, some women volunteers were recruited to sell the products directly to their friends and neighbours on a house to house basis. The products were an instant success. Then came the crunch at the end of the first month when the retailers started demanding the shades that got sold, the distributors went out of stock for the popular shades and new stock could not come as the earlier bills for the chemicals was not paid. Retailers were ready to pay for only the new bill and not the old bill, so the distributor was not ready to clear the remaining payment (he had paid only 25% of the amount) and the sales stopped.

The moment the new stock of the in required shades was not supplied, retailers refused payments for even the stock that was sold and the total operations were stopped. The distributor somehow recovered his money by selling the stocks at rock bottom price to wholesalers.

End Result: Product planning, market research and the introduction were done very professionally, but because of financial restraints the product failed to remain in the market.

So do not plan business without having adequate financial support.

Questions

1. Do you think that SWOT analysis was done before entering this project? What would the SWOT suggest?

2. Do you think the research was done properly?

3. What strategy would you suggest for success?

Case Study – 9

MORE NAVY CUT KINGS SIZE FILTER TIPPED

Japan Tobacco International, the world's third largest cigarette seller after Philip Morrison (Godfrey Philip's parent company) and British American Tobacco Co. (ITC's parent Co.) entered the Indian market as a buyer of tobacco for their operations in other parts of the world, with their office at Hyderabad. The company saw that the Indian cigarette market was dominated by ITC (Indian Tobacco Co.) with over 80% market share and GPIL having roughly 12-15 % market share and the remaining was with VST (Vazir Sultan Tobacco Co. - Charminar), Dunkan's Tobacco Co. (Rothman's) etc. The company saw a big opportunity in the Indian market. India had not yet accepted WHOs (World Health Organization) dictates to ban advertising and promotions of tobacco products and so was showing a steady growth rate of 6% annually, as against a drop in the sales of major markets of the world.

In India, Maharashtra and Karnataka had a high urban population with the habit of cigarette smoking and expendable income. Other parts of India had young population having the habit of chewing tobacco and eating 'Khaini' or 'Gutkha' and those who smoked tobacco preferred cheaper brands of cigarettes of 'Bidi'. So it was decided to have Pune and Bangalore as test markets. They opened their sales office at Bangalore with their Indian subsidiary, JT International India Pvt. Ltd. The Pune market-combing operation was entrusted to the author while the market-combing operation in Bangalore was done by the company sales staff.

The Bangalore market had consumers speaking mostly Kannada language and for others, without understanding Kannada language, survival became difficult without understanding the local language as most of the people in the southern states of India refuse to accept our national language Hindi for political reasons and do not understand English. Thus it became important that the advertisements and promotions had to be done in Kannada language. So Pune was replaced by Mangalore as the test market and Mysore was selected as another market in place of Bangalore. (for similarity with Mangalore).

Product Development: It was found that ITC's Bristol was the largest selling cigarette by volume, but its India Kings was the highest selling cigarette by value in both Navy Cut and King's size segment. So it was decided that the cigarette to be launched would be in both navy cut and king's size segment and the brand would be "More" as it was a known brand in India for many years in the form of cigarillos (long thin cigarettes) in various flavors.

Market Testing: The product was market tested several times in the Bangalore and Pune markets, with many smokers being given one week's free stocks of cigarettes (no brand or company identification) and were interviewed to find their acceptance to the cigarette. It was found that all these smokers who were regular smokers of India Kings started liking their cigarettes when the taste and flavor of the product was matched with that of India Kings. When the product was blind-tested, 90% of the consumers said that it was India Kings cigarette.

Product Pack Design: In the in-depth interviews consumers were found to be associating their smoking habit as a symbol of fun loving, outgoing character and the selection of the brand as a symbol of status. So the pack design was decided to be bright red colour with golden lettering.

Advertisement Testing: Since the consumers were of a fun-loving and outgoing nature, the advertising campaigns were designed to be based on fun and outings. Most of the promotions were planned at major discos, bars, in restaurants and pool table clubs.

Distribution Strategy: ITC operated with salesmen working on commission basis and the salesmen were not paid any salary. They operated with a box carrying cigarettes and other products on a fixed route. They sold the stocks to retailers at a suggested selling price during the day, making two or three rounds to the major outlets on the same day and returned the balance stock to the distributor in the evening along with full payment for the stock sold, deducting their commission of 0.8%. The salesmen visited only the major retailers (whom they offered credit of one to two weeks) and medium size retailers that paid money readily. The other retailers purchased their requirements from wholesalers. Salesmen covering major routes earned more than Rs.10,000/- per month through the commissions.

The initial expectation of the market share was only 1% of the total market in the given cities. Suresh suggested that the company appoint one salesman for every six routes on salary basis, where the salesman would visit all major retailers once every day (number would be very small) and for others, twice or once a week. To make it easy to visit a larger area, it was planned that the salesmen would be given a cycle with a box in Mysore and Mangalore, and moped (Bajaj M50) in Pune and Bangalore and the money would be recovered from them in EMIs (equitable monthly installments) from what was due to them. The boxes would be painted red in color and carry the brand logo in gold and the salesmen would be given red T-shirts with brand logo and a red baseball cap.

Suresh suggested that the distributors be asked to appoint sales staff at salaries ranging from Rs.3000/- per month to Rs.5000/- per month for salesmen, Rs.5000/- to Rs.7500/- per month for the supervisors and in addition they should be given incentives on achievement of a target fixed daily allowance to take care of petrol expenses etc. To ensure that good distributors with enough financial strength and infrastructure accept the work, as the monthly turnover was expected to be low, they should be given ROI guarantee of 24% per annum to be calculated every quarter.

The test launch in Mysore and Mangalore was a success with hoardings at prominent places with many shops having display boards and the successful sampling operations and promotions like free gifts and tickets for discos etc. The product captured more than the expected 1% market share. Elated with the success of the Mysore and Mangalore launch, the company planned an extension of the products to Pune and Bangalore markets with similar promotional plans within the next three months. Suresh appointed CFAs (clearing forwarding agents) in both Bangalore and Pune and recruited and trained sales staff also at both Bangalore and Pune. The launch was scheduled for March 2003.

More shiny disco balls,
More Jennys from the block.
More lights to turn off.
More D.I.S.C.Os.

Fig. 1.7: Invitation Card for "More Fridays" in Popular Pubs in Bangolore, Mysore & Mangalore

Launch of Pune was handled by Suresh. He selected the best of the locations for hoardings and for kiosks on the street light poles (famous amongst them were MG Road and Bund Garden bridge), promotions were arranged at discos like 'Appache' 'Scubadoo" 'Screem' 'Fulora' etc. and all five star hotels. Sampling was arranged at all Puneri Kattas (with a declaration by the consumer that he is over 18 years of age etc.) and the launch was a grand success in both Pune and Bangalore.

Then came the advertisement ban on tobacco products in May 2003 and everything went down the drain. Without advertisement and promotional support and consumers yet to shift loyalty to the new product, the product sales started dropping and within the next six months, came down drastically. The company had to close most distribution points and keep only one distributor working with few salesmen. By the end of the year, the company withdrew the stock and closed shop.

Result: Without advertising and promotional support, a product cannot generate trials and get the loyalty of customers at the entry of any new product, so the product failed.

Questions

1. Was the strategy to appoint salesmen on salary basis right? Why?

2. Was the strategy to appoint salesman for six routes right?

3. What do you thinks is the reason for failure?

Case Study - 10

READY DELIVERY OF AROMA PRODUCTS

Aroma Products, a major name in cosmetics and personal products, had a large market share and was the market leader. Their competitors were becoming very active and since many of them were local players with much smaller units manufacturing, their products had price advantage due to zero excise duty being paid. Because of this, these competitors gave higher margins to the retailers and a longer credit period. Aroma Products had a large consumer base loyal to it and the best of quality standards to affirm the customer's trust in it. Aroma Products had a three level distribution channel with CFAs (carrying and forwarding agents) in all the states and distributors in all the towns, and multiple distributors in large cities. The distributors supplied the products to retailers after orders were booked by sales officers every week. The western region was divided in five areas under area sales managers viz. Mumbai city, rest of Maharashtra, Gujarat, Madhya Pradesh and Chhattisgarh. Mumbai contributed to almost 35% of the sales, the rest of Maharashtra came second with 30% sales, Gujarat with 15%, Madhya Pradesh with 12% and Chhattisgarh with 8%. Recently it was found that in Mumbai city sales were declining slowly while Maharashtra grew at the fastest rate. Other areas showed steady growth but nothing spectacular. Madhya Pradesh and Chhattisgarh had a major problem of illiteracy amongst the consumers who were easily cheated by retailers and had been given spurious products having similar sounding names and high retail margins.

Mr. Partho Choudhury the new regional manager was worried as the major contributor to the sales-viz Mumbai was declining without having any major competitor. He called in Mr. Abhay Kanetkar, the Maharashtra Area Sales Manager to his cabin one day. During the monthly meeting Mr. Choudhury asked him whether he would be interested in working in Mumbai as ASM. Mr. Choudhury felt that only a new ASM could have made a difference in the sales approach and make a turnaround and start growing. Mr. Kanetkar accepted the challenge and gave a positive reply.

The interchange transfers were carried out immediately and Mr. Kanetkar took charge of Mumbai city the next day. The first thing he decided was to meet all the Mumbai distributors numbering six, one by one. Since Mr. Kanetkar had worked in Mumbai city as a sales officer earlier, he knew all the distributors personally and so decided to visit them on his own, without having a sales officer accompanying him. He visited all the six distributors in the next three days and went through their DO (Delivery order) book and payment register found the following:

1. Many orders booked by Sales officers (SOs) were getting cancelled.

2. Retailers were giving post-dated cheques for even smaller amounts.

3. Many retailers were signing on the bill and promising to pay in the next week (credit bills).

4. There was a lot of damaged stock with the distributors as no Damage inspection reports (DIR) were made regularly and completely (SOs made DIR only for a maximum of 2% of the turnover.

5. Stock registers were incomplete and were not signed by SOs periodically.

6. POP (Point of Purchase) was lying in warehouses and was being misused by distributors.

7. All the distributors were unhappy with the working of the SOs.

8. Pipeline stocks were higher than stipulated by the company reducing the distributor margin to a large extent.

The next step of Mr. Kanetkar was to work with the SOs, and so he concentrated on finding out why the orders booked by SOs were getting cancelled. He worked along with the SOs, and alone to find the right reason for the orders getting cancelled. He found the following-

1. According to the SOs, the distributors delayed order supply and it was being sent only after two or three days. Meanwhile, the retailers bought stocks from the wholesale market and refused the deliveries.

2. According to the retailers, the SOs promised replacement of damaged goods but the distributors refused to do so. So they had no option but to return the goods or sign the bill and not pay.

3. Many retailers said that the distributor was not supplying to them as many bills were pending and they were willing to pay if all the damaged goods were taken back.

Mr. Kanetkar next checked the total DIR reports for the whole of Mumbai and found that actually the quantity was not very high, but because the reports were not being prepared regularly, it had accumulated to a large quantity.

In his next weekly meeting with the SOs he asked them whether damaged goods replacement was the only problem they faced and if the problem of damaged goods was sorted out would the business grow?

The SOs came out with another problem where they said that the distributors were giving priority to deliveries of other company products for which they were having distribution rights and their earnings from those companies were higher. This problem was manageable if the pipeline stocks were rationalized, as the margins given by both the organizations were the same and just because the pipeline stocks were high and damaged stock was not cleared the investment was going up and the ROI was going down. He had to ensure two things

1. The distributors would send the deliveries in time.

2. The distributors would replace damaged stocks from the market when SOs asked them to do so.

Both the things could be ensured if the distributor gave a working van to the company SO along with his billing person and delivery man. This would ensure that the deliveries were made on time, replacements were given and SOs could display the goods themselves thus increasing visibility and sales.

He called a meeting of his SOs and asked them to work out the van expenses. The SOs were not interested in the working of the van as it would tie them to the market for a longer time. But Mr. Kanetkar insisted on the method on a trial basis and to be continued if found profitable for both the company and distributor. The SOs said that the vans working expenses were between 1.5 to

2% of the monthly turnover. Mr. Kanetkar thought that if the investments were rationalized, the distributor ROI would go higher than their expectations, and they would concentrate on the business of AROMA and thus the business would start growing. He decided to talk to his RSM and get the following permissions-

1. Issue credit notes for the damaged stocks with the distributors at one go.

2. Reduce the pipeline stock by taking a cut in primary target for one month.

3. Give these facilities only to those distributors who were willing to give a working van.

Questions

1. Do you think the plan will be acceptable to the RSM?

2. Would this help in improving the sales?

Case Study - 11

HAIR-SHINE SHAMPOO

SKACO Company was marketing various cosmetics in India, with many of the products being market leaders. One of their products, 'Hair-shine',- a shampoo with conditioners had been a market leader with around 70% market share. For the last two years, this product had not shown any growth and was losing its market share to new products being launched by competitors, with an image of youthfulness. The product was expected to lose sales volumes further as the consumers perceived the product as old-fashioned and for the previous generation. The Marketing VP, Mr. Khanna along with Mr. Mane, the CMD had called a meeting of the Group Product Managers looking after various product lines. Mr. Katkar who was the Group Product Manager for hair care products was also present. They wanted to take a decision about 'Hair-shine' that day with the following options-

1. Allow 'Hair-shine' to die by stopping all the expenses on it and reap the profits as long as possible.

2. Introduce a new youthful product with attractive packaging to replace 'Hair-shine' which could compete with new products of the competitors.

3. Re-launch 'Hair-shine' with a new attractive packaging and additional ingredients/variants to attract the new generation also.

The following facts were available to the people who joined the deliberations for the meeting.

1. Allow 'Hair-shine' to die and reap the profits by stopping the expenses

The Finance Director, Mr. Jaju was of the following opinion, for the following reasons

- The product being a premium product with high volume production, had a very high profit margin and earned a huge profit for the company.

- The expenditure on the product had shown no significant gains in terms of product volumes and actually reduced the profit margins.

- Since the product was being used by consumers in the age group of 30 onwards, the segment was large and not easily willing to change the brand in use. So the product was expected to give good profits for at least another 20 years or more, if only good displays at the point of purchase were maintained and an occasional reminder advertisement.

2. Introduce a new youthful product with attractive packaging to replace 'Hair-shine' that can compete with new products of the competitors.

The people who supported this option also supported the first point of allowing the product to die a natural death in the course of time. These people had the following arguments in support of their option.

- A new generation product can include consumers in the age group of 15 years onwards, giving a large consumer base.

- Since television advertisements coverage has now reached rural India through satellite dishes

(DTH transmission), a large chunk of the rural consumers could also be enrolled who are not using 'Hair-shine' currently.

- The new generation is seen as more fashion-conscious and less price-oriented and so the new product with very attractive trendy packaging could be sold at a much higher price than 'Hair-shine'.

- The new generation advertisements can use the latest fashion divas to promote the product.

- The new product would have a better distribution and it would be available easily and instantly as retail support would be available along with 'Hair-shine'.

- The product was expected to turn around in less than three years.

- Cannibalization would not lead to loss of customer base, as the old customers would shift to the new product of the same organization.

- Re-launch would not allow high pricing as the existing customers may resist high pricing and so gradual price upgradation would be required.

3. Re-launch hair-shine with new attractive packaging and additional ingredients/variants to attract the new generation also.

The following points were forwarded by the supporters in favour of re-launch of "Hair-shine" with a modern outlook

- The re-launch would lead to all the existing consumers getting converted to the new product instantly.

- High volumes of the product would be assured from the beginning.

- Retail support would help re-launch without any problems.

- High volumes would ensure the economies of scale leading to a low production cost and high returns.

- The re-launched product would attract the younger generation along with the older generation.

- No new manufacturing capacity would be required to be developed as the same facility would manufacture the new product.

With all the parties having strong support arguments, the decision has become difficult. Will you help them decide by selecting the option for them, by giving the reasons for the same?

CHAPTER 2

Cases in
Retail Marketing

Case Study - 1

ICE-CREAM FRANCHISEE

Radheshyam Bansal was looking for franchisee arrangements with a reputed international ice-cream giant. The ice cream company had the following terms of business-

1. A minimum of 2500 sq. ft. shop area in a high-income group residential area.

2. Furniture as per the company design by company-approved contractor.

3. Storage of one week's inventory with all the varieties being stocked.

4. No replacements for the products.

5. Franchisee not allowed to sell any other products, even if they are not in competition, in the same premises.

6. Advertisements by the parent company in the newspapers and on national TV.

7. No ROI guarantee to be given by the company.

8. The company offered 15% profit margins with an expected annual turnover of Rs.30 lakh.

9. Franchisee should have one manager and one helper in the store.

10. Electricity bills were expected to be Rs.5000/- per month.

Radheshyam had such a place available with him where the monthly rentals were Rs. 25/- sqft.

Should he accept the terms of the franchise? What terms should Radheshyam negotiate for?

Solution: Radheshyam should not accept the franchisee even if the brand is very big world over, as the conditions in the western world and the Indian sub-continent are totally different. We can list a few of them as follows:

- In the Western world, land and real estate are comparatively cheaper (non-scarcity item).

- Customers in the West are habituated to a lot of moving space and like large areas.

- There is no fixed MRP system; and so every shopkeeper can have his own markup so the products are sold at whatever rate is commercially viable for the shopkeeper.

- There is no fixed wholesale price, and so the shopkeeper can negotiate on the basis of quantity purchased and the displays arranged.

- All the shopkeepers have their own markup and so the same product is available at different prices in different shops.

- Returns on the investment depend on customer footfall and not on the margin available. If fewer customers are available the markup is high to compensate for low turnover.

- Competition is not fierce as in India.

Western brands should not expect Indians to accept terms that are prevalent in their countries. Radheshyam cannot get even 10% ROI with such conditions and may end up in losses.

He can accept the terms only if he is trying to set up business for the next generation and allowing them to handle it and learn. The losses can be treated as training expenditure as he can then change the business and run some other profitable business at the same place.

Questions

1. What should be the minimum ROI a franchisee should get? Why?

2. What should be the minimum area of shop for an ice-cream parlour considering Indian conditions?

3. Do you think American companies need to study Indian conditions properly before entering Indian markets?

Case Study - 2

AKBARALLY'S CHEMBUR

Manoharlal was interested in investing money in the retail business and was looking for a suitable place. While traveling through Mumbai he saw the closed departmental store Akbarally's at Chembur and was interested in buying the entire place.

The place had the following plus points-

1. Large infrastructure with furniture.
2. Large warehousing place with parking for goods vehicles.
3. Large parking place for customers.
4. Location with a large display frontage on an ever-flowing traffic on the main artery in Mumbai.
5. Affluent clientele residing in the nearby area.
6. All licenses available only needed to be transferred to the new owner's name.
7. Centrally air-conditioned shop floor.

Manoharlal wondered why was the establishment had closed down with losses in spite of all these plus points. The reasons he found through various people were-

1. All the products were sold at a high profit margin to cover the expected rate of returns on the investment.
2. The earlier owners expected a high rate of return on the floor area also.
3. They charged extra amount for gift-wrapping of the products.

4. Many products carried a note – 'Specially made for Akbarallys' and had a high MRP than the nearby stores.

Manoharlal looked into the business generated by Akbarally's and the possible business with competitive rates and found that the break even was possible within seven years, with competitive pricing and considering the rate of property appreciation. Manoharlal was looking for a break even point in five years.

Questions

1. What according to you, should Manoharlal do? Give reasons.

2. If the rate of appreciation of property is more than 25%, should Manoharlal invest in the said property?

Case Study - 3

KACHAROOMAL FIGHTS SHOPIN

Kacharoomal Dungarsi was running a retail provision store that was started by his grandfather. The store was large with 100 feet frontage and around 300 sq. ft area and high ceiling with mezzanine. Recently, the area in which he was operating saw a lot of developments and new towers started coming up. A new shopping complex was also coming up, where many branded product showrooms and restaurants were about to open. In one section of this shopping complex, an all-India retail chain 'Shopin' selling provisions, vegetables and grains was coming up. Shopin was known to give customers a rare experience in shopping with fresh vegetables and fruits cleaned and packed in refrigerable packets at competitive rates, but were selling provisions at MRP and grains at market rates. So the customers were expected to shift to Shop in for self-service counters, with a spread of products displayed in air-conditioned comfort, and cheaper vegetables and fruits. The disadvantage with Shop in was that they offered no credit and home delivery to customers and their timings were from 9am to 8pm.

Kacharoomal was worried about the fate of his shop and did not understand what to do. One day he met Mr. Kalsekar who was a great friend of Kacharoomal's father and was the Area Sales Manager for some MNC selling FMCG goods and was now working as marketing consultant. Kachroomal called Kalsekar to his shop and requested him to suggest some ways to ensure that his shop survived and grew in spite of the onslaught of the retail chain. He also offered consultancy fees to Kalsekar.

Kalsekar told him, "Give me two days, and I will give you suggestions such that not only will your shop survive, but it will also be impossible for Shopin to earn profits.

After one week, Kalsekar came with the following suggestions-

1. Convert the shop into self-service mode, but continue the current practice of accepting monthly lists and home delivery.

2. Create a ramp to reach mezzanine floor with shopping trolley; as this will increase the shopping area.

3. Start opening the shop at 6 AM and keep it open till up to 11 PM and, let the staff work in two shifts.

4. Fix CCTV cameras in the shop to keep a watch on both, the shoppers and the staff, to avoid shop-lifting.

5. Create display windows on the complete frontage of the shop and rent them to big MNCs at a good rent.

6. Fix fridges for cold storage of various ready-to-eat snack foods.

7. Accept telephonic orders of regular customers and offer credit to them.

8. Ensure that all major brands are stored in your shop and avoid unknown brands for the sake of high margins.

9. Maintain a good quality in provisions and other products.

10. Maintain good relations with all the customers.

Kachroomal accepted all the suggestions as it only required that he do the changes in the furniture set up and fixing of CCTV cameras. He was already running his shop from 6 AM to 11 PM. He could get MNCs to hire the windows for display and found that it could get him a lot of money every month. The business of his shop went up and he started feeling secure. After some time, Shopin closed down and an electronics product showroom came up in its place.

Questions

1. What is the reason for the success of Kacharoomal?
2. What do we learn from this experience?

Case Study - 4

PESHWAI JEWELLERS

The fourth generation of the Patwardhan family was in the jewellery business which was established in Pune in 1860, and as the family expanded they established their shops in Mumbai too. One of the branches of the family established their shop in San Jose in California and the name Peshwai Jewellers became famous in USA too. Prakash Patwardhan was looking after the San Jose shop and was sourcing his jewellery from their shop in Prabhadevi, Mumbai, where his brother Pradeep was looking after the business.

Many of their customers were ordering jewellery in India for delivery in the USA and vice-versa to take advantage of the online service. Prakash was keen to establish an e-business through catalogue sales and capture the market in Europe, Canada and the Middle East initially, and then in far eastern countries where the Indian population was growing and there was scope for growth. He started looking for a marketing consultant who would do this work effectively and they finalized Prism Consulting, an India based marketing consultancy with operations in the Middle East and Europe. Prism Consulting, after studying all the aspects of the business came up with the following points-

1. Since the price of gold was volatile and differed in USA and India, there was a need for standardization and also a firm pricing policy needed to be fixed to change the pricing of products, based on the market price of gold. They suggested the following two options-

    a. The price should be changed every 15 days in the catalogue and the rate should be as per the catalogue.

    b. The price should be charged as per the local gold rates on the date of the order being placed and payment to be done accordingly.

2. The location of the distribution centre is a very important factor, and to avoid double taxation, the distribution centre needs to be located at a tax-free, neutral place where local taxes will not be applicable.

3. The catalogue needs to be available on the internet in 3-D format with classification of the jewellery.

4. Making-charges have to be fixed on the basis of the design intricacy and the number of gems being fixed, and not on the weight or price of the jewellery as is the practice everywhere.

5. Delivery time has to be fixed on the basis of geographical locations of delivery and nowhere should it be more than two working days.

6. The cost of the distribution centre will need to be apportioned to each and every item sold and for that, a firm sales forecast needs to be done, based on consumer research undertaken in various parts of the world by developing contacts with the Indian population in those parts.

7. Peshwai Jewellers must work out the costing of all these points and find out whether the e-business will be commercially viable.

8. To reduce the cost of the distribution centre, there is an option of opening a jewellery store in a tax-free location like Dubai in the Middle East.

Peshwai Jewellers weighed all the options and found that the idea of selling online jewellery across the globe, in the current situation was not practical. They had to continue doing business as they had been operating previously and accept orders based on the catalogue placed on their website, without any price tags and delivery time declared. That way they could keep doing business and sell products that were available off the shelf for immediate delivery. For other products, they could specify the time required as per the order given by the customer. Here, they could charge the customer at prevailing prices. Delivery charges were to be separately charged.

Questions

1. Do you think Indian laws are conducive for export business? What changes would you expect Indian Government to implement to increase exports?

2. Do you think to start mail order International business reputation of the business house is of paramount importance?

3. To ensure delivery in 48 hours what location in the world is most suitable? Why?

Case Study - 5

PLAN WELL TO GAIN WELL

'For-U' a superstore in a middle class locality was started in the year 2000 by Chaganlal Chedda whose three generations were in the business of retailing of provisions. Chaganlal's younger son, Paresh, who did his MBA in marketing from a reputed Institute was not interested in joining the traditional provisions business and aimed at retailing in the Western style where he would be an MD and his GMs would handle the day-to-day affairs. Chaganlal Chedda had two sons and the elder son, Ramanik was already helping him in the provision store that had a large clientele which was being serviced by home delivery system, through 50 delivery boys. The delivery boys, along with some other staff cleaned, graded and packed the provisions regularly for supply to their customers. The provision store, Chedda and Co. had a large retail outlet of 2000 sq. ft. and in addition to this, had a warehouse of 6000 sq. ft.

Chaganlal agreed to Paresh's request and purchased 20,000 sq. ft. store area with 10,000 sq. ft. of warehouse-cum-office area for Paresh where he created a self-service retail shop with four check-out counters. Paresh recruited experienced staff from 'Suvidha' (which was closing down their business in Maharashtra) and a manager called Mr. Chopra from another retail chain. The retail store was named 'For-U' and opened with much fanfare.

Chopra had promised Paresh that he would ensure profits in the first year of the store operations and he proposed a lot of promotional activities in the store which are listed below-

1. All the major newspapers should announce the opening of the store with a half- page advertisement.

2. A celebrity would inaugurate the opening of the store.

3. Loyalty programs would be devised.

4. There would be weekly discount days (every Wednesday).

5. Lucky draws in the first week of every month would take place where customers would get refund of the entire money he/she paid for that day's purchase.

Chopra got in touch with various organizations producing packaged commodities and foods to get extra quantity discounts, so that they could be passed on to the customers on Wednesday. For the first few months, the store did well with high footfall, but started losing customers afterwards and had very low business even during festival months. They ended with a big loss at the end of the first year. Chaganlal asked Paresh to look in to the matter and take corrective steps before it was too late. Paresh had meetings with Chopra and the other staff on how to improve the situation. Chopra insisted that the steps he was taking were right and Paresh must wait and watch for another year for improvements. Paresh agreed to this as he also looked into the workings and found them correct.

However, Chaganlal was not willing to wait. He discussed these matters with various area managers of reputed FMCG companies, and all of them said that there was a flaw in the business plan made by Paresh and Chopra. Chaganlal then got in touch with Mr. Nagarkar who had started his marketing consultancy after opting for VRS from an MNC selling FMCG products. Nagarkar visited 'For-U' and came back to Chaganlal saying that there were a lot of changes that were required to be done and he was willing to do them if authorized to take action. Paresh resisted the move and said, "What will an FMCG Sales Manager know about retail business?" But Chaganlal insisted on appointing Nagarkar saying that "An FMCG Sales Manager has more understanding of customers and business profitability." He asked Paresh to give Nagarkar three months and if they found that he was making positive changes, then they could continue. Paresh agreed to this proposal.

Nagarkar came with the following proposals and changes-

1. Start a grains section because it was a volume business with a home-delivery option.

2. Grains should be graded into various qualities and prices for everyone to choose from.

3. Stop the purchase of all unknown brands in packaged foods and liquidate existing stocks by giving it to wholesalers at purchase price or at a one-time loss.

4. Create display windows on the front side of the shop that could be rented to various organizations.

5. Start renting display positions (eye-level shelf spaces, corner display units, neon signboards inside the shops etc.).

6. Rearrange shop spaces with grains and provisions at the back and vegetables and fruits

at the beginning, along with refrigerated items like frozen snack foods and bakery items.

7. Create a separate section for cosmetics and rent a part of the section to a major cosmetic company as shop-in-shop (SIS).

8. Reduce the prices of all the soft drinks, tea/coffee, chocolates and snack foods where the margins are high and sell these products at slightly below MRP and run quantity purchase schemes (QPS) for purchase of these products (Take the help of the manufacturers for the same).

9. Start a system of purchase monitoring and inventory control.

10. Fix CCTV cameras with the monitor in the office, monitoring the customers and staff activities.

11. Conduct a training programme for staff on customer relationship.

12. Start motivational schemes for the staff for getting a higher billing.

Nagarkar said that the first and foremost thing was to reduce the inventory of unwanted products, control inventory of wanted products and attract customer footfalls. The second most important thing was to create a regular fixed income that would take care of the establishment cost, either fully or to a large extent. Chaganlal gave a go-ahead to Nagarkar, and he found that in the first month itself, Nagarkar reduced the inventory to one fourth level, saving a large cost on inventory. Chopra was asked to go, saving another lot on the salary front.

The training on customer relationship conducted by Nagarkar was a hit and there was a marked difference in the staff's working, as they became more customer-friendly. The CCTV nearly ended shop-lifting and workers idling and chatting, thus increasing their efficiency. The end of the first month saw some employees getting rewarded for good work. Since more customers came in for the purchase of soft drinks, fruits and vegetables and bakery products which were available at a competitive price, they purchased other products also along with these. The grains purchase, though at lower margins, ensured higher turnover. In all, the first month showed working profit which was not there earlier. The working profit encouraged Chaganlal and reduced the apathy from Paresh.

In the second month, the SIS for a major cosmetics company and all the display windows and other spaces getting rented out had ensured a profit for 'For-U' , as the rent from all of these was more than the recurring expense, and it largely covered the salary cost also. Since the customer footfalls increased drastically, the store was on its way to profitability and Nagarkar said he was sure to reach BEP by the end of the third year and start generating book profits.

Chaganlal explained to Paresh that following the western method blindly would not help in any business in India. Indian conditions were different, Indian customers were different, their expectations behaviour were very different. We must understand the customers to satisfy them, give them quality products and understand business economics for success.

Questions

1. Do you think the failure of many organized retailers is due to blindly following American system? Why?

2. What is the difference in behavioural patterns of American and Indian consumers when it comes to purchase of daily need products?

3. What is the difference in Indian and American environment?

CHAPTER 3

Cases in
Industrial Marketing

Case Study - 1

PATHARE OEMs

Prakash Pathare worked as a Factory Works Manager for auto ancillary products manufactured by a German automobile company. The products manufactured by the company were important OEMs in most of the automobile companies and were being used by all the brands of automobiles, in all the categories (passenger to commercial vehicles). These products were easy to manufacture, once the moulds were ready and the machining was perfect. Most of the automobile companies imported these products and paid a higher price along with import taxes, therefore these indigenous products would be sold at much lower prices and still earn high profits.

The major problem Mr. Pathare envisaged was of getting an Industrial plot near to Pune that would not increase the investment levels and marketing of these products to the customers under the new brand would be easier. He could get such a plot on Paud Road in a privately developed industrial estate. The plot had electrical connections, water connections, an industrial shed and an office already constructed. The previous owner was selling it because he was unable to raise the required funds and was unable to sustain the unit.

Pathare started visiting various customers under the guise of a customer survey and secretly enquired with them about their willingness to purchase the same quality products at lower rates from an Indian company. All of them showed willingness only if the quality was equivalent and the results of the trials were satisfying. Pathare got hold of a draftsman and prepared the product designs, without altering the major features. Since the designs were not patented he could go ahead with getting the machinery installed and moulds made. Once the foundry was installed, he resigned from his existing job. The organization refused to release him before he completed his notice period of three months. This actually helped Pathare to collect trial orders and make the required changes as per the customer's requirements.

Pathare supplied his first order in the very first month of the opening of his industrial unit and was flooded with enough orders for the entire year. Pathare fixed his pricing at 30% lower than the imported product and was able to clear all his loans in the first year of operations.

He has now started exporting the product to Europe and many Asian countries and has established himself strongly as an auto ancillary supplier. Now Pathare wants to develop some more products and increase his business to higher levels.

Questions

1. What was the business strategy used by Prakash Pathare? Why was he successful?

2. What additional product range would you suggest to him for business growth?

3. What marketing organization structure would be appropriate for his efforts? Give reasons.

Case Study - 2

LALCHAND FASTNERS

Lalchand started looking after his father's business of manufacturing fasteners of various sizes and types after completing his MBA. The initial months went only in understanding the business nitty-gritties and then he started attending the monthly sales meetings. In the first meeting he attended, he sat next to the Sales Manager and listened to all the discussions making notes but saying nothing at all. The very next day he called the Sales manager and asked him the following questions.

Fig. 3.1: Industrial Fasteners

1. Do we have annual targets for every executive? Have executives divided these annual targets customer-wise and month-wise and submitted them to the office?

2. Is there no system of comparing the achievements with the same month in the previous year?

3. Is our sales figure declining as against last year/ targets?

4. If the sales are declining in any particular area, have we compared the sales achievements customer-wise?

5. Are there any particular customers who are showing a decline in sales?

6. What corrective actions have we initiated to restrict the decline in sales at any customer point?

7. What is the distribution channel designed for our products?

8. How many competitors do we have?

9. Which competitors sell their products in excess of our volumes/value?

10. What is the reason behind competitors being able to sell more quantity/ value?

The sales manager was a very trustworthy person and known to Lalchand's father. He had been working for the organization almost from the beginning. He asked Lalchand to give him a time of 15 days to compile all the information as required by him.

At the end of three weeks, the Sales Manager was able to give him the following answers-

1. Monthly targets were discussed every month in the meeting and were based on the previous month's achievements.

2. Annual targets were prepared every year at the company level and given to the executives as their guidelines, but the executives did not divide them customer-wise/ month-wise.

3. Achievements were compared with the previous month and the months target but not with the previous year for the same period/the target for the period.

4. The sales were declining as against the previous year and also the yearly target.

5. No comparison had been done customer-wise but he had asked all the executives to do the comparison before the end of the month when they came for the monthly meeting.

6. They would know the customers that were showing a decline at the time of the monthly meeting.

7. They would start taking corrective actions after the meeting.

8. They sold products through their area-wise selling agents, who in turn sold to their customers. In some areas, they sold directly to the customers without any area selling agents.

9. They mainly had only one competitor.

10. His sales were growing continuously and that was affecting their sales. He used to sell lesser quantity than them till the last year but had recently started selling more quantity as compared to them. There were a few local manufacturers but as compared to them, they were lower in quality and had negligible sales volumes.

11. Their competitor was selling directly to the customers and gave them more margin.

Lalchand went to his father Surajmal and discussed the matter and said, "We have only recently fallen back as compared to the competition and our goods are still very good. I would like to personally go and find the reasons for a drop in sales and find out solutions for the same. I have plans to add some more products and a new foundry with the latest technology, but for that we must regain our market leadership and start growing."

His father was very happy with his enthusiasm and said, "I am happy that you are interested in the family business and want to grow it. I was not looking for any growth as I was not sure whether you would join the family business. Now, you do what you want to do, but ensure that you discuss with me before any major decision is taken."

During the next monthly meeting, the following facts were unearthed -

1. All the area selling agents were showing a decline in sales; the drop in sales was due to their customers not buying expected quantities as earlier.

2. Area selling agents were not having proper manpower to give weekly coverage to end dealers. They said the lower turnovers were making it difficult to keep more sales staff.

3. The area selling agents were asking for sales staff allowance. Currently, they were given 20% margin, out of which they gave 15% to their customers and 5% they kept as sales staff cost and transportation.

4. The end dealers were giving preference to the competitor products as they were getting better margins in them.

5. End dealers said that the selling agents were not supplying stock regularly, as they clubbed all the orders together and supplied once in 10-12 days. For emergency, they were required to send their own vehicle and pick up stocks, thus reducing their margin.

6. All the dealers wanted to supply directly, as they could give better results.

7. The customers buying stocks directly were showing a growth in sales.

8. There was no incentive to complete targets.

Questions

1. What actions should Lalchand take to improve the situation?

2. What actions should Lalchand take in relation to the sales executives?

Case Study - 3

THE TEA/COFFEE MACHINE

Mr. Redke was an Industrial Safety Commissioner based in Pune, having only one son called Adinath. He was not interested in studies and had not completed any degree or diploma . Redke was worried about Adinath's future. Though Redke was wealthy with a lot of agricultural land, a house in Pune and Solapur, Adinath could have a good life even if he did nothing except looking after the agricultural land. Adinath had no interest in agriculture and wanted to enjoy a good life in Pune. There was another problem. He wanted to get married and good proposals were not coming as he was not employed. Redke wanted to get Adinath settled in some business venture before his retirement in two years, so that he could find a good bride.

Redke's relative, M. S. Siddhanath had started manufacturing Tea/Coffee Vending Machines and the required tea/coffee ready mixes in Karnataka and wanted to have some agent in Pune. Knowing that Redke was an Industrial Safety Commissioner he felt that it would be easy to get contacts in the Industries around Pune and establish a good business. He approached Redke with a proposal for starting a business for Adinath. Redke liked the idea and replied positively to Siddhanath and started looking for a marketing consultant who could prepare a proper plan and help establish the business. Redke met Nagarkar in a function and was impressed by him. Nagarkar accepted Redke's offer to establish the business for Adinath.

In the very first meeting that took place at Redke's residence in the morning, Adinath was absent as he was still sleeping after a late night outing. So Redke, Siddhanath and Nagarkar had initial discussions about the strategy to approach various industries, the pricing to be offered and the product brochures to be printed and their design. Since Siddhnath was already having product brochures that he was using in Mysore and Bangaluru, it was decided to use them with the required modifications. Redke promised to have them ready in one week's time and Nagarkar said that he would come up with the list of prospective industries where they could approach to get the machines installed.

Fig. 3.2: Tea/Coffee Vending Machine

In the next week, again when Nagarkar met Redke at his residence before he went to office, Adinath was sleeping due to a late night party, so they discussed about the different industries and the arrival of the demo machine with tea/coffee powder for sampling. The machine was expected in one or two days and the tea/coffee packets had already arrived. So it was decided to have the first call next week after the machine was tested for demo.

It was another ten days before the meeting with the HR manager of a large industry on Solapur Road near Indapur was arranged. The meeting was at 11.30 am and so Nagarkar said that they could start comfortably by 9.30 am and reach by 11.00 am. The industry manager had arranged a luxury car from Kent Cars (since Adinath was the Safety Commissioner's son) and the car and Mr. Nagarkar were ready by 9.00 am, but by the time Adinath could wake up and get ready, it was almost 10.30 am and by the time they actually started, it was nearing 11.00 am, so Redke informed the industry manager that his son was expected to reach by 12.30 pm and that the manager should wait for him.

On the way, Adinath took a halt at Indapur for breakfast and by the time they reached the Industry premises it was 1.30 pm and the manager had left for lunch at home and then for a meeting in Pune. He had made arrangements for a good lunch for Adinath at the canteen and his assistants were instructed to have a look at the demo of the machine.

The same thing happened in all the subsequent industry visits and Adinath never followed-up with the industries that were contacted. Nagarkar suggested that Redke appoint sales executives, as Adinath was not willing to make any efforts. The industries were also delaying decisions as they knew that Redke was nearing his retirement and may go on pre-retirement leave.

Nagarkar, through his persuasion could procure three orders for the machines and got them installed but Adinath was not willing to do anything. The enquiries stopped the moment Redke retired, as Adinath did not approach any company on his own. The venture was closed down, as by that time, both Nestle and HUL had come out with their machines and ready mixes which had better market acceptability due to their established brand names.

Questions

1. What went wrong in the sales promotion?

2. Why did Redke's good relations not help in getting business?

3. Was Adinath's lethargy at fault or was it the Consultant's mistake?

Case Study - 4

THE CASE OF PHOTOSENSITIVE SWITCHES

Arun was looking for a job in sales, but he had no previous experience and training in sales, though he had a good personality and was willing to work hard. He was a good communicator also. He saw an advertisement in the newspapers and appeared for the interview. He got shortlisted because of his good communication in Hindi, English and Marathi, the local language. The salary offered was not good but Arun knew that he needed the experience of working as a sales representative to get any good job, as good jobs were open to experienced people only.

When Arun joined the company, he came to know that their main business was not selling photo sensitive switches but the owner had taken this agency for his son Mukesh, who wanted to have his own separate venture. Mukesh was given a separate cabin but was required to use the common office staff area for the time being. Arun was the only sales -representative for the entire Mumbai metropolitan area. The job was to sell photo-sensitive switches that operated on light. Mukesh showed him the demo kit where a switch was fitted on a board with a bulb and a wire, with a plug that could be connected to power. When Mukesh put his hand against the switch, since it sensed darkness, the light was switched on and when he removed his hand, the light went off. Mukesh explained that the switch was useful to reduce manpower required to put on and off the lights in the industry, on the roads etc.

Mukesh had no experience in marketing and asked Arun to start establishing contact with various industries and explained the instrument. Arun started out without a price list, brochures, information on the company and the clients that were using the instrument. Actually, he was not aware that customers would demand this information. He started with an industrial estate close to one of the suburban railway stations and started meeting the owners/managers of the industrial units. Most of persons were interested in knowing about the instrument, but not in purchasing it, as their small industrial units had no need for such instruments. Arun was happy meeting various people and talking to them about the instruments and he had a feeling of achievement and was reporting to Mukesh about the meetings and contact details of the persons visited and the demo given. Mukesh was very happy with the efforts and gave Arun a raise in his daily allowance that he was demanding. Arun spent more than two weeks visiting all the industrial units in that compound numbering more than 100. At the end of more than two weeks, Arun met the owner of a unit who he had met on the first visit to the industrial estate. He said to Arun, "You are still here in this compound? No one will buy your instrument here as our units are small and some of the workers nearby switch on and switch off the lights. So go visit a bigger industry!"

In the fourth week after starting work, Arun started visiting the bigger industries. The modus operandi was simple and he would take a bus to the Belapur Industrial area and visit the industries there. He used to approach the industrial units and at the security gate he would ask for an appointment with the purchase manager. The security would promptly send Arun to the reception area and the receptionist would ask him to wait. Waiting in the reception area was a good experience as Arun could sit in air-conditioned comfort and read various magazines that were kept at the reception. Sometimes the purchase managers called him early and sometimes they made him wait for long hours. In such cases, they allowed him to have lunch in the factory canteen at subsidized rates. Arun used to be very happy on such occasions as the lunch was available at a lesser rate than a cup of tea outside. The purchase managers used to see the instrument and send Arun to the factory managers for technical viability. Sometimes they would ask him to come the next day after making him wait there for many hours. Arun would not mind coming again as the prospect of getting a big order was before him, with all the industrial units spread on many acres of land with many facilities in the open area, with thousands of tube lights. That was the time when Arun came to know that in all the chemical factories, everything needed a Safety Certificate from the Industrial Safety Commissioner's office. So Arun asked Mukesh to get the Safety Certificate from the Industrial Safety Commissioner's office. Mukesh asked Arun to do it so he went to the Industrial Safety Commissioner's office and gave the application along with the sample of the switch. He came to know that it would take many months to get the certificate and so he started carrying the application copy along with him saying that the certificate was expected. Some of the factory managers told him about the timer switches that were being used to switch on the lights at 7 pm and switch them off at 7 am. These switches were very commonly being used, but they had a drawback of the setting time for winter and summer, when the sunset timings differed.

Arun had worked for more than four months in the company without procuring a single order. Then one day he received a call from a multinational FMCG company and got selected as his confidence was very high and he had a good experience, though for a short duration.

Questions

1. Why was Arun not able to procure any order?

2. Was the company's induction training to Arun adequate? Give reasons for your answer.

3. Was the organization well-prepared to handle the sale of the instrument?

4. As the owner of the company, what would be your preparation before you started selling the product?

Case Study - 5

POLYVINYL PIPES

Sagar Shirole had joined a company manufacturing polyvinyl pipelines and fittings, mostly used in chemical companies to transfer corrosive chemicals from one place to another. The pipelines and fittings needed to be replaced every time there was a maintenance job being carried out, as most of the time, the fitters were unable to remove the joint properly and were forced to cut them. These pipelines were also used for water sprinklers in farms and for drip irrigation purposes to some extent. The company had created goodwill amongst the clients and had a fixed business on a regular basis. But Sagar had no potential for showing his selling skills as it was a fixed business and so the scope of vertical growth in the organization was restricted.

(a)

(b)

Fig. 3.3 (a) & (b) : Polyvinyl Pipes

Sagar went to see his marketing professor, who was himself a very successful Sales Manager in the FMCG sector. He said, "Sir, I do not find any opportunity for vertical growth in this organization as there is no scope for volume sales growth."

His professor said, "Sagar you are forgetting the basic principle of sales growth. Don't you remember?

More customers,

More number of times.

More quantity,

For getting higher sales volumes?"

Sagar said, "Sir, I do remember the basic principle, but we are already covering all the available customers and there is no chance of them buying more quantity. In fact, some of the clients are shifting their production units to an area where the land prices are low and the Government is offering higher subsidies and tax benefits. This will actually reduce the sales."

The professor asked, "What will come in the place of these production units?"

Sagar said, "Residential and commercial buildings."

His professor said, "Then go and start selling to the builders."

Sagar asked, "Sir, are you joking?"

"No," said the Professor, "Remember the formula for B2B selling? -

S - Survey/suspect

P - Prospect

A - Approach

N - Need development/negotiations

C - Close of call

O - Order processing

"We already suspect that the builders may use the plastic pipes; the only question is to develop the need for them and start approaching them."

Sagar was still confused. Then the professor explained, "Builders use various types of pipes in construction work. Mostly, these pipes are-

- GI pipes - for water connections and internal wiring.

- Cast iron pipes - for drainage lines on the building.

- Concrete pipes - for underground drainage lines.

You can always ask them to use plastic pipes in place of GI and cast iron pipes, as this will save them a lot on cost, without sacrificing the Quality

"But Sir, how will I convince them to use plastic pipes?" Sagar asked.

"Use the FAB (features, advantages and benefits) Analysis effectively," the professor said.

Sagar was very happy that he had met his professor. He prepared the FAB Analysis and started getting in touch with various builders. The FAB Analysis was as follows:

1. Features of the Product-
   a. Lightweight
   b. Available in all sizes
   c. Non-corrosive
   d. Long- lasting
   e. Economic

2. Advantages over competition (traditional)-

   a. Merges in the wall colour and looks good.
   b. The thieves cannot climb on these pipes, so there would be lesser number of house breaks.

3. Benefits-
   a. Reduces the cost of fittings.
   b. Reduces the cost of labour, as the plumber needs only one helper.

Initially there was a resistance to the use of plastic, but when a big builder constructing a low -cost housing society decided to buy the pipes, others followed suit.

Sagar reported the highest growth in the sales volumes consistently. He was promoted to the Area Sales Manager position ahead of his seniors and was also rewarded for creative selling techniques that benefited the organization.

Case Study - 6

HOTEL SUPPLIES

Ambalal Mutha's father was running a cloth shop in Kapad Peth at Sangli. At the beginning of the 1960s he found that many people were going in for the power loom business to manufacture cotton saris and bed sheets. Since the saris and bed sheets manufactured on power looms were much cheaper than saris and bed sheets manufactured by bigger textile mills, even the textile mills were willing to buy them from power loom owners and process them further for selling them at higher prices. The Maharashtra Government was offering a lot of subsidies and tax breaks, as Sangli was an under-developed zone. Ambalal's father took a wise decision and established a textile shed with eight power looms.

When Ambalal completed his education, he joined his father's business, being the only son with three sisters. Ambalal sold the saris and bed sheets through his own cloth shop in Sangli and through the shops of his brothers-in-laws at Pune, Mumbai and Nagar, and business was good and profitable. Then a change came in the late 1990s when a powerful minister from Ichalkaranji encouraged the power loom sector in Ichalkaranji and many people shifted their business to Ichalkaranji with the latest versions of power looms. After the closure of the textile mills in Mumbai, Bhivandi and Malegaon, Ichalkaranji got government support and the business progressed there, thus leaving Sangli much behind Ichalkaranji.

Ambalal also shifted his looms to Ichalkaranji, as it was becoming difficult to get labour in Sangli. His business progressed, with four showrooms of his family members, and so sales was not much of a problem. The condition changed further in the new millennium when ladies stopped using cotton saris and shifted to polyester saris and salwar suits, and the business of saris dropped. Ambalal was forced to stop manufacturing saris and increase the quantity of bed sheets. Selling bed sheets required him to search for clients other than his family members and he was forced to sell at a very low price and give extended credit where he was earning almost nothing.

In a chance meeting with Mr. Omprakash, in a marriage ceremony in Pune, Omprakash suggested that Ambalal should meet his friend who was the Sales Manager of an FMCG company, Mr. Nagarkar and take his advice. Omprakash arranged meeting of Ambalal and Nagarkar the next day and Nagarkar said that he would definitely get back with some good suggestions.

After surveying the market, Nagarkar came up with a suggestion that the hotel industry was growing and they constantly required bed sheets, tablecloths and curtains with their logo either woven or printed on them. Ambalal would need a sales team that would visit the various hotels all over Maharashtra and procure orders. To start with, Ambalal could utilize the services of MBA students doing their summer projects. Nagarkar was a visiting faculty at some of the management institutes. He could select bright students for this purpose and Ambalal would need to pay them handsome allowances and commissions. Nagarkar said that he could supervise the projects of the students and ensure that they got good business.

Ambalal recruited four students and divided Maharashtra among them, and asked them to get the orders. The students, under the able guidance of Nagarkar got a good amount of orders and listed many prospective buyers with their contact details. Nagarkar asked Ambalal's son to supervise the marketing operations later on and recruit two sales executives to do the job. Ambalal then started supplying crockery and cutlery also to these hotels along with bed sheets, tablecloths and towels. His business is now well-settled and growing.

Questions

1. What was the strategy adopted and suggested by Nagarkar for Ambalal?

2. What was the mistake Ambalal had made in his business outlook?

3. What do we learn out of this case study?

Case Study - 7

SUPPLY OF KITCHEN EQUIPMENT

The International Institute of Management Studies decided to start a Hotel Management course, as it was gaining importance and a lot of students were opting for it. The requirement of the course was very simple. It was as follows-

1. One kitchen of 30 sq.m. area
2. A restaurant with a bar counter
3. One guest room, complete with all furniture (bed, wardrobe, TV, sofa, and washroom).
4. One reception counter with a lounge.
5. Usual classrooms

Setting up the restaurant and bar, guest room and reception was easy as the furniture was readily available, but setting up of the kitchen was the major problem as the equipment manufacturers made equipment to order and nothing was available off the shelf. Mr. Vashishth, the Director and Mr. Bansal, the Chairman of the institute set out searching for suppliers of kitchen equipment locally, as the equipment suppliers available on the internet specialized in equipment for large hotels with international standards and were very expensive. For an educational institute, the equipment was not required to be of international standard. It was only required to be of workable variety and strong enough to remain in working condition after the rough use by the trainee students.

First, they got in touch with the marriage hall people who had equipment tailor-made for their own use and kept getting it replaced or ordered additional equipment. Most of the people said that they got equipment from their own workshops and that they were the suppliers of equipment to other marriage halls and many restaurants. After establishing contacts, most of the hotel owners also gave them the same reply, and Vashishth and Bansal began to wonder who was the manufacturer and who was the user, as all the people claimed to be both, manufacturers and suppliers. They decided to ask them to give quotations for setting up the complete kitchen that would have the capacity of cooking food for 100 customers. All of them were not able to submit the quotations in the given time limit, as many of them were not the manufacturers, and they had to contact the manufacturers to get the quotations first and then add their own commission, to arrive at the price to be quoted. This exercise took some time and Vashishth advised Bansal that they would not take any decision for some time and if the suppliers called, then they could be told that they were reconsidering the decision to start the Hotel Management institute as the initial cost was turning out to be very high.

A month passed and one day one of the suppliers, Mr. Rajendra Sopal came to meet Vashishth at the institute. His business card read, 'Manufacturers and suppliers of kitchen equipment' and the address was of an industrial estate nearby. Sopal said that he had heard that they wanted to start a Hotel Management institute and he was interested in setting up the kitchen and supplying the equipment. He also added that he was the supplier of kitchen equipment to all the marriage halls and many hotels in and around the city. Vashishth asked him the first question on why he had not got a website for himself? Why was he not available in the yellow pages? Sopal answered that he was so busy manufacturing and supplying the equipment that he did not think of going in for a website and the yellow pages, as no matter who took the order for equipment, it finally came to him to be manufactured.

Vashishth found that the rates quoted by Sopal were 30-40% cheaper than all the quotations received by them. Sopal was given the order to set up the kitchen and supply all the equipment.

Questions

1. Was Sopal right in his views?

2. What advice would you give to Sopal to increase his business?

3. Why do you think Vashishth decided to prolong the release of the order?

CHAPTER 4

Cases in
Service Marketing

Case Study - 1

JOSHI ENTERS THE HOUSEKEEPING BUSINESS

Joshi intends to open up a housekeeping company in Pune. Currently the business is being handled by three major companies having offices all over India and they amount to nearly 60% of the potential business. Only one company has its own manpower and machinery and the other two operate through sub-contractors who use company-owned machinery. The sub-contractors are paid very low wages that do not take care of even the minimum Government stipulated wages and welfare such as PF and ESIC benefits.

Fig. 4.1: Joshi Enters the Housekeeping Business

The machinery required to clean the toilets and windows (internally and externally) costs an investment of about Rs.20/- lakh which was seen to be a major entry barrier for new entrants and the other barrier was an educated, English speaking and communicating person to coordinate with the company officers.

Joshi's business plan shows that he can generate good profits with three years turnaround on investment, even at 20% lower rate quoted to the clients.

The major points in his business plan are-

- People are unhappy with the work efficiency and the attitude of the cleaning staff on roll.

- The cleaning staff on roll take many leaves and mostly on Mondays, creating hygiene problems in the office.

- No one wants to oversee the work of the cleaning staff on roll as they back- answer in foul language.

- Changingthe cleaning staff is a big problem as they start fighting with the newly-appointed cleaning staff and created law and order problems.

- Many times, the cleaning staff threatens the office staff of false police complaints under the Atrocity Act.

- The administrative staff is happy to deal with someone educated, but are not willing to spend more money as demanded by the reputed housekeeping service companies.

- Housekeeping service companies are favoured as they supply a replacement if the regular staff is absent.

- There are thousands of companies interested in such a service but which are going untapped.

Joshi's pricing at 20% lower than the established companies, is slightly higher than the cost of the cleaning staff on roll, but promised hassle-free service. The only problem Joshi saw was that of getting a loan for the equipment. He got in touch with the equipment manufacturing companies and enquired whether they were willing to supply the equipment on installments but they refused. Joshi's friend suggested that he should contact MCED (Maharashtra Centre for Entrepreneurship Development). MCED asked him to do a small course in entrepreneurship and registered him with the DIC (District Industries Centre). With both, MCED and DIC supporting Joshi, he was promised a loan by a nationalized bank.

Questions

1. Should Joshi invest in the machinery and enter the field?

2. What kind of marketing organization would you suggest to him for success?

Case Study - 2

GM HOUSEKEEPING SERVICES

Guruprasad Mandke was working for the last six years with a housekeeping services company and had acquired all the knowledge of its working and then had decided to start his own company, GM Housekeeping Services. He started with his own bank account in the company name that required a shop act licence and professional tax registration. He talked with some of the labour contractors that supplied him labourers when he faced staff crunch, and took their lowest rates to begin with. He got in touch with the companies that were not being serviced by his current company and decided to resign after he got his first order contract. He started quoting rates that were nearly 20% lower than the company he was working for. This way, he was sure to earn more than his current salary, even if he got only one company to begin with, since he was not going to appoint any supervisory staff and he was not liable to pay any PF, ESIC benefits to his staff, his salaries would be lower than the current company.

Guruprasad was sure to get contracts from at least one company immediately and start his business by Gudi-Padwa, the Hindu New Year day and an auspicious day to start new ventures. But even by the time of Holi he did not get any response from any of the companies he had given quotations to. He was worried and started calling the HR managers of these companies and asking them why they were not considering the offers. Most of them said the offers were not workable and he needed to reduce the rates after having negotiated them to a workable level. Guruprasad could not understand and decided to have negotiations with one of the HR managers to understand the real problem. So he called up Sachin Deshpande, who was his distant relative from his wife's side.

Sachin Deshpande was an experienced HR Manager with many years of work experience, and so he suggested that Guruprasad set up a meeting at any quiet restaurant on any weekday except Wednesday, Fridays and Saturdays when all the restaurants are expected to be crowded. Guruprasad set up a dinner meeting on Tuesday immediately in the next week.

Sachin Deshpande asked Guruprasad what was the basis that he decided his pricing on?

Fig. 4.2: GM Housekeeping Services

Guruprasad said that he was charging 20% lower than the price quoted by his current company and it was accepted by most of the MNCs. This price gave him comfortable margins that ensured that he received a good monthly income for himself.

Sachin Deshpande said that that was not the way the price was decided. The prices were decided on the basis of what the customers were willing to pay.

"But customers will always want to pay negligible amounts," Guruprasad retorted.

"No, customers will pay the amount that is profitable to them but will make sure that the service provider earns; otherwise they will not be able to get any service provider," said Sachin. "There has to be a win-win situation," Sachin added.

"How can there be a win-win situation, when the companies tried to squeeze the service providers?" Guruprasad asked.

"A service provider should not try to get all his profits from one company, he must earn it through several clients by dividing his load of expenses on several clients," said Sachin Deshpande. "Ask me why I should employ a service provider instead of my own employees?" Sachin Deshpande added.

Guruprasad kept quiet. "Ask me why I should employ a service provider instead of having my own employees?" Sachin insisted.

"Why should you appoint a service provider?" asked Guruprasad.

"Before I give you the answer, I want you to think about it loudly. I will help you in finding the answer," Sachin said. **Guruprasad started listing the reasons for the appointment of a service provider-**

1. Reduce the salary burden.
2. Ensure that the work is done professionally.
3. Ensure that the work is completed before the office opening time.

4. Ensure that the windows are cleaned from inside out.

5. Ensure that the fans, furniture etc. is properly cleaned.

6. Ensure that deodorants are sprayed regularly.

7. Ensure that the telephone instruments are cleaned and scented pads are inserted and regularly changed in the mouthpiece.

"Is that all?" asked Sachin.

"Yes, these are the reasons I can think of immediately," said Guruprasad.

"Barring point number two and three, everything is not so important. A task master office administrator can get it done without fail," said Sachin.

"You are missing the most important point," he added.

"And what is that?" asked Guruprasad.

"The most important point is that these people keep taking leave without permission and that it can be for any number of days. In their absence, who would clean the toilets was the major question, as we want undisturbed service on every working day without fail. A service provider will always ensure a replacement," said Sachin.

"Let me tell you the story of my friend who was working in an MNC. The sweepers were absent on the day a foreigner was to visit the office. The entire toilet block was stinking because it was the first day of the week and the toilets were cleaned on the last working day of the previous week in the morning. Since the foreigner was part of the TOP brass, my friend lost his well-paying

MNC job," said Sachin. "MNCs can pay to avoid such situations," Sachin further added.

"Now what do you want me to do?" asked Guruprasad.

"Rework pricing, calculate all your expenses with reasonable profit percentage and don't forget to consider PF and ESIC, as it is the contractor's responsibility to pay, even if his staff is less, because his staff is considered to be a part of the client's staff and get the benefits. If you don't do the deductions from your staff's pay, the client will deduct it from your payments and then you will be required to pay both, your contribution and the employee contribution," Sachinsaid.

"I will sign a contract with you and ask few of my few friends from the HR association to do the same," Sachin added further.

Guruprasad thanked Sachin profusely and said, "I feel I should have done a management degree at least by correspondence to understand these details. I will do the needful and I am sure you will find my rates proper and thus lead to a win-win situation."

Questions

1. What were the mistakes of Guruprasad?
2. Do you think a management degree would have helped?
3. Do you get all the knowledge through books of management or was it Sachin's experience that made the difference?

Case Study - 3

STAY-WELL GUEST HOUSE SERVICES

Ajay Bhave had two bedroom flats in Mumbai and both these flats were located near Andheri in suburban Mumbai, in the same building and on the same floor. He had purchased these flats during the early nineties when the real estate rates in Mumbai had dropped due to the serial bomb blasts. Ajay was working in the USA then and he thought of buying these adjacent flats where he could stay with his parents, when he came back from the USA. His parents were staying in Matunga in a rented two-bedroom apartment since his father's childhood. After he purchased these two flats, his father's building underwent re-development and his father could get a three-bedroom flat in the same building on nominal payments.

Ajay came back to Mumbai in 2002 after the Y2K (year 2000, change of millennium) requirements of software personnel were over. Getting a job according to his salary expectations was difficult in Mumbai and he didn't want to shift to Bengaluru or Hyderabad where many new software companies were getting established. Since there was no option at hand, he accepted a job in Bengaluru and started staying in a PG (paying guest) accommodation. He had enquired in Bengaluru schools for admissions and found that admission to a good school was difficult and required lot of donations. In addition, unlike Maharashtra, all southern states are compelled to study the regional language even in convent schools. Studying Kannada would be difficult for his high-school children and the school they were studying in Mumbai was a most-renowned one.

He and his colleagues were required to visit Mumbai frequently for meeting clients in BKC (Bandra-Kurla Complex) area in Mumbai. Since he had his house in Mumbai he could comfortably stay at home while in Mumbai, but his colleagues faced a lot of problems in getting reasonable accommodation in the allowances given by the company and most of the time, they spent out of their pocket. Because of this, they were agitated with the organization and were demanding higher allowances to stay in good hotels in Mumbai nearer to BKC. Ajay came to know from his friends from other organizations that they also had similar problems and that was affecting the business of many organizations in Bengaluru as they tried to avoid sending staff to Mumbai.

Fig. 4.3: Stay Well Guest House Services

One day Ajay's HR manager asked him if there was any guest house known to him that could be hired on a monthly basis, where 3-4 persons could stay and get breakfast and dinner at reasonable rates. Ajay asked him as to what would be the monthly rent the company was willing to pay and what would be the charges of breakfast and dinner. The HR manager said that the per day expenditure per person of staying in Mumbai was currently Rs.4500-5000, and on an average, 3 persons are expected to stay in Mumbai for around 12-14 days. That was working out to be approximately Rs.2 lakh a month. He could get a very good rental flat fully furnished for Rs.60-70000 around Andheri, but having a caretaker would increase the cost to above Rs.1 lakh. Getting a good trustworthy caretaker was a problem. Some of the star hotels were offering service accommodation at Rs.1.5 lakh a month. So if he could get any guest house for Rs.1 lakh he would be willing to take it immediately projects were starting within three to four months and they needed a guest house urgently. The guest house could sometimes accommodate more than 4 persons also.

Ajay was currently getting Rs.20,000 as rent from each of the flats and the lease was about to be renewed in that month. As he wanted to change the lease, he had asked them to vacate the flats that month. He told the HR manager that there was such a place and it would be ready to be hired in a month's time, provided the company made a contract for at least five years and gave one year rent as deposit. The HR manager could tell him the furniture requirements in the guest house. The HR manager asked him to negotiate the terms with the owner and then he would sign the contract at the end of the month. Ajay got both his flats furnished like a guest house as he could get it leased to another organization on the same terms. He arranged for one caretaker at Rs.10,000 per month common to both the flats and signed a contract with a nearby Udupi restaurant for the supply of breakfast and dinner as per the telephonic order given by the caretaker.

One year passed off well, with Ajay making good money through the guest houses for which he had floated a private limited company. But in the second year he started getting complaints about the linen not being properly laundered. Ajay checked with the laundry bills and found that the bed sheets and towels were being sent to the laundry everyday even when guests were not occupying the rooms. He also got complaints that sometimes when the guests reached unannounced; some other persons were staying there. He also got complaints from his society that the flats were being used as a card-playing club on Sundays when no guests stayed in the guesthouse. Ajay's wife said that she was not in a position to keep a constant check. Ajay's aged parents were also not in a position to check and the appointment of a manager was also not going to solve the problem. Ajay started searching for another caretaker to replace the current one.

In the meanwhile, Ajay got an offer from a Mumbai-based organization that was paying a much lesser salary than that of the Bengaluru-based organization. But he would save on PG accommodation and other expenses and would get to stay with his family. In addition, he could keep a proper watch on the guesthouse's working and maybe add one or two more companies, as he would then be in a position to purchase some more flats in the same locality and possibly in the same building.

Questions

1. What should Ajay do? Should he change his job and go to Mumbai?

2. What precautions should Ajay have taken to avoid the complaints?

3. What can he do to compensate for his loss of salary by coming to Mumbai?

Case Study - 4

TRINITY MOTORS

Trinity Motors operated a showroom for trucks and LCVs for a company which was the market leader for more than 40 years and had a monopoly for these trucks and LCVs in the entire western Maharashtra. After liberalization, the company lost business to newer entrants due to better marketing and improved versions of the trucks that carried better load at higher speeds and had better amenities like power steering and comfortable cabin designs. The company kept on losing their market share and came down from 90% to less than 40% because of this. Trinity Motors also lost a huge amount of business.

Fig. 4.4: Trinity Motors

The company introduced sports utility vehicles and had instant success. This improved the business volumes of Trinity Motors but because of high competition, their profit margins reduced and their net income went down. The management of Trinity Motors announced incentives to their marketing and service staff for increasing business volumes that could lead to a higher net income. The

Marketing staff started visiting various tour operators and various corporate offices to increase the business and started getting reasonably good success. The service staff however was falling short of their targets. They then came out with the idea of increasing the profit through higher sale of spares to their customers. They started replacing spares, even when not required, thus increasing the business. Since the profit margins in spares was higher than vehicle sales, they were able to achieve higher profit margins. This went on for a couple of years and Trinity Motors was in a good situation.

After a few years, Trinity Motors found that the income through the services was falling and Mr. Kalke, their General Manager started analyzing the reasons for it. The reasons were startling! Customers were purchasing vehicles from them but getting them serviced (even the free services) from another dealer who had recently started his showroom in another part of the city. Mr. Kalke employed first year MBA students and asked them to do a survey and find out the reasons for it and all the customers said-

1. "You take longer time to service the vehicles."
2. "You change spares unnecessarily."
3. "Service quality is questionable

Questions

1. What actions would you suggest to Mr. Kalke for improving the image of Trinity Motors?
2. How will they win back their lost customers?

Case Study - 5

RK IMAGING SERVICES

Rakesh was worried about his business, as this was the third time his client had been annoyed with him, and he did not know what the problem was. Rakesh was running a software service for an advertising agency, where his job was to download the various images from the internet and mix and match them according to the client's requirements, to form new images that were required by his clients in various presentations and print advertisements. His client base was various advertising agencies, printers and OOH (out of home) advertisers. Rakesh himself was a very skilled worker on these requirements and was known to deliver all the jobs that he accepted on time. After his training in the job, his wife Kumud joined his organization. Along with her, he employed one more staff member who could do the job of downloading the required images and add-on to the images bank that Rakesh had created over a period of time. This helped him go out and meet his clients personally to seek additional business.

Fig. 4.5: RK Imaging Services

His business had started growing, but his delivery schedule was getting disturbed. His initial assessment was that because he himself was spending lesser time on the job and his wife was slower in the work, the work was getting delayed. So he started spending time at the office after office hours to prepare the required images for the clients and then he found that the required images were not available all the time. He was required to spend most of his time downloading the required images and then proceeding for the actual work. He talked to his wife Kumud and asked her to check on the work done by Abhijit, the staff member he had employed for downloading the images. Either he did not understand what was to be downloaded or else he was spending more of his time on social media sites and not giving enough time for the job at hand. Kumud said that Abhijit seemed to be as incere worker but she would have discussions with him and see to it that the required images were downloaded in time.

Next week again, Rakesh was trying to complete his work and found that the required images were not available in the data bank, even when he had particularly told Abhijit and Kumud that it was important to have the required images downloaded without fail. The next day he decided to have some hard talk with Abhijit and went to the office in the morning. The moment Abhijit arrived, Rakesh called him to his cabin and started firing. Abhijit listened to all the talk and then finally said, "I have been asking you take a leased line to improve our connectivity and you have not done anything. We changed the internet provider three times in the last one year i.e. from MSNL to SOCOMO to Speed Tail but the service of all of them is bad. They promise one speed, but in reality, we hardly get even50% of the promised speed. The speed is so slow that it takes hours to actually find the required images and then an equal amount of time to get them downloaded. Either we should install a leased line or reduce our business."

Rakesh was in two minds whether to go in for the leased line as the initial payment was very high. Or should he reduce the workload? One more alternative was not to accept urgent assignments, but then, urgent assignments paid him double the normal rate.

Help Rakesh take the perfect decision.

Questions

1. What is the main problem in this case? Is it the connectivity or is it the slow rate of staff working?

2. If Rakesh takes lease line will his problem be solved? Explain how.

Case Study - 6

MAULI PLACEMENT AGENCY

Dnyaneshwar, popularly known to friends as Mauli, after the famous saint of Alandi, completed his MBA in HR and was looking for a job in a good organization. He found that most of the bigger organizations had computerized most HR functions and because the labour unrest had died down, organizations had cut down on labour welfare officer posts. The work in the HR department was now that of recruitment (due to high attrition rates) and training. In recruitment also, to reduce the cost of recruitment, most companies went in for placement agencies (no more head hunting, they wanted people at the lowest and middle level continuously). So job opportunities in most organizations for HR persons were limited and Mauli had to look for a job in a recruitment agency.

Fig. 4.6: Mauli Placement Agency

Mauli started calling on various recruitment agencies for jobs and he found that the salaries offered by these agencies were extremely low and they all promised to pay incentives on billing. The incentives were high but paid only after the recovery of the bill and that happened after 3 to 6 months, depending upon the contract the agency had for replacement of the selected worker in case he/ she left within that period. The bills came in promptly from the organizations that were recruiting continuously (high growth and attrition rates) and were delayed by organizations recruiting sporadically. To recover the bills, the agency owners bribed the HR personnel of the recruiting organization, thus reducing the net recovery and so the incentives. He found that some of the agency owners harassed the employees and made them leave the organizations under the pretext that they were not completing the targets and avoided paying incentives to them.

Some of the recruitment agencies were found to be taking a high amount of registration charges and promised the job seekers three interview calls. The job seekers were given calls for any post that was not even suitable for the job seekers or some calls were given at the eleventh hour, so that the job seeker could not attend it. After three calls had been given, the job seekers were asked for re-registration. Some of them even asked the job seekers to go through aptitude tests from a particular agency where the charges were very high because the agency got a hefty cut from it. Most of the job seekers were shown to be on the border line of the job they were interested in and were asked to enroll for training for the aptitude test for the job, through the same agency and the same hefty cut for the placement agency. This aptitude test racket many times involved placement coordinators of educational institutes who made money out of that. Mauli disliked the complete process but could do very little about it.

Somehow Mauli was lucky enough to complete his targets and stay for a longer time in each agency he worked for and shifted with an -increasing salary package for himself.

Mauli developed good relations with various HR persons, who also disliked the rot that had set in the recruitment process and was advised to start a clean recruitment agency that they could use for their recruitments.

With the Internet becoming common and many job portals registering CVs free of charge, more and more job seekers were registering themselves on these job portals. These portals allowed recruitment agencies to download these CVs for a fee but offered the classified CVs in various ways so that the recruitment agency could download CVs as per their requirements and then shortlist candidates for sending them to the recruiters. The only problem was that the same CV could get forwarded to the recruiter by more than one placement agency. The other problem was that many job seekers got their CVs made by professionals and so they looked very good but actually were duds. So a placement agency needed to call the candidate for an interview at their office first, before forwarding the CVs to any recruiters. Job seekers avoided giving an interview to the placement agency that was charging a registration fee and an agency not charging registration fee had a better chance of screening and selecting better candidates, and so their candidates had a higher chance of getting selected.

Mauli decided to use a procedure where he would not charge registration fee from the job seekers and employ good recruiters at high incentives, which were definitely paid to the recruiter. Soon Mauli started getting the best of the recruiters as his employees and some of them brought good industry contacts with them, leading to more organizations recruiting through Mauli's placement agency. Mauli's became a leading placement agency in a few years.

Questions

1. What jobs were available to MBA HR pass out students?

2. What problems were faced by the new recruiters?

3. Why was Mauli able to attract good recruiters?

4. Was it right on Mauli's part to be so liberal?

Case Study - 7

RK TRAVELS & TOURS

Rajkumar Malhotra started as a travel ticketing agent for a reputed tour operator and subsequently went in for starting his own bus service, after he could get financial assistance and procure a loan for purchasing a 30 seater luxury bus. He started operating it on a route that was not operated by any of the major travel companies, but had enough passengers willing to pay a higher amount for the luxury of the A/C and thus, run one trip a day. He had calculated the fare with 30% occupancy rate and cost plus profit basis and in actual effect, he could get nearly 70% occupancy rate regularly and 100% in vacation periods and on weekends as it was location for a weekend picnic.

RK Travels & Tours

Fig. 4.7: RK Travels & Tours

While running his own bus on the single route, he was working as a ticketing agent for many other tour operators. He found that all travel buses came from Mumbai and picked up passengers travelling towards Bengaluru. These buses reached at his location in the late evening and reached Bengaluru the next day (late morning). His passengers always looked for any bus that could start in the afternoon or early evening and reach Bengaluru early in the morning, before the morning rush hour started. Since the number of travelers was good, he thought of starting his own service that could start early in the evening and reach Bengaluru early in the morning. The problem was that he needed to have two buses and not one, so that he could operate the service every day from both the sides.

The banks were willing to give him a loan as his credibility had gone up after clearing the earlier loan in time and operating his accounts in the same bank. But the loan installment was high and it would exhaust his entire earning out of the operation and more if the occupancy rate failed. The long route service required two sets of double drivers and commission to the ticketing agent in Bengaluru, that was required to be higher than other tour operators who managed their own offices in both Mumbai and Bengaluru. Rajkumar planned one trip to Mumbai every day during the day and made similar arrangements at Bengaluru to make one trip to Mysore after reaching Bengaluru and avoid idle time. These additional trips ensured that Rajkumar earned a small profit after paying for maintenance and loan installments on both the buses.

Rajkumar went on to purchase another set of buses as he found that the better timings were attracting higher passenger density and so he went in for one more set of buses that started in the early morning and reached in the late evenings. Since morning service was not available from any of the operators, he could get 100% occupancy at the same rate. Within a short time, he was a major bus operator on the Mumbai–Bengaluru route. He asked his son Rahul who was in college to help him so that he could start some more routes like Mangalore and Hyderabad. But his son was more interested in partying and roaming around with friends. His wife used to say that he should enjoy his youth and that he would take responsibility when it fell on him.

Rajkumar fell ill and was diagnosed with cancer. He had to undergo surgery and then chemotherapy and could not attend office. His son was forced to take charge of the operations. Rahul went to office whenever it was absolutely necessary and asked their manager to keep running the show as his father was doing. He went on signing blindly on the papers that the manager brought to him. Rajkumar was indisposed for more than a year and one day, he received a call from his garage owner for non-payment of bills. He also he received a call from the gas station for pending bills for fuel. He called his son Rahul and enquired about the bills. Rahul said that he had signed the cheques for the bills and there had to be some mistake. Rajkumar decided to go to the office at least for some time to see what had gone wrong.

When Rajkumar started checking, he found that large amounts had been withdrawn from the bank and no account or explanation was available for its use. The occupancy had reduced to nearly 50%, there were a lot of complaints of breakdowns. Rajkumar called the drivers, and found that most of the old drivers had been removed and new drivers had been were recruited. The old drivers said that the buses were going full but there were two types of tickets being segregated and accounted for. They also said that bus tyres needed replacements as they were worn-out. Rajkumar saw the purchase bills for new tyres from a new supplier and was surprised to see the tyre conditions. He could see many fuel bills paid in cash to unknown gas stations, which was not supposed to happen. He called his agents in Bengaluru, Mysore and Mumbai, and they said that the manager had told them that he had become a partner in RK Tours &Travels and so 50% of the tickets were to be paid separately in his name. They had tried to talk to Rahul but he could not be reached and whenever he answered, he said that whatever the manager was doing was right.

He called the manager to his cabin, and the manager said thathe hadanexplanation for everything and would show all the records in an hour's time. Afterwards, Rajkumar came to know that the manager had left the office without telling anyone. Rajkumar called the police station and registered a complaint of fraud against the manager.

Questions

1. What went wrong in RK Travels &Tours?
2. How could this have been prevented?
3. Was Rahul at fault? How?

Case Study - 8

FAST-FOOD RESTAURANT CHAIN

SKACO Company is a world-renowned company having fast food chains across the globe. Recently they had decided to enter the Indian market and they had already formed a JV with Raman &Co, a Chennai-based company already having a chain of restaurants in Tamil Nadu. The SKACO product range is equivalent to KFC and has various popular dishes both, in the vegetarian and non-vegetarian sections. The price range of products starts from Rs.60/- per dish to Rs.240/- per dish depending on the choice of the ingredients and veg. / non-veg. selection. The Chairman of SKACO Company had called a meeting that day to decide on the marketing strategy. The CEO of the JV, Mr. Kapoor, along with the CMD of Raman &Company, Mr. Venkat Raman and the VP of Sales and Marketing, Mr. Shetty were the other members present in the meeting. They had the following options to consider:

1. Start a chain of restaurants like Kamat's and spread across the state, having presence in every district place.

2. Open restaurants only at state capitals.

3. Open restaurants at all major cities including state capitals.

4. Open restaurants only in theme tropolitan cities.

Fig. 4.8: Fast Food Restaurant Chain

The following facts had been circulated to all the members of the decision-making group

- People in the South are price-conscious and only affluent people are willing to spend more money in fashionable restaurants for a style statement.

- Maximum business can be expected from people who are interested in eating quality breakfast.

- Peoplewere willing to spend money only if a liquor bar was available; this restricted the number of outlets.

- Software professionals were willing to go to fashionable places and spend more but they were available only in Bengaluru, Mysore, Mangalore (all in Karnataka), Hyderabad in (AP), Chennai in (TN) and Cochin in Kerala. In all the rest of the places, the income levels of the people were low and they could not be expected to patronize such stores.

- Middle-income group people went out to have snacks (tiffin) and lunch/dinner (Sapat/Utta) with families, but preferred South Indian specialities only.

- The working middle class preferred self-service restaurants (standing at the counters and eating) where South Indian specialties were served and sambhar and chatniwas given in unlimited quantity, and the rates were low.

- North Indians staying in the South preferred sit-down places but frequented South Indian specialty restaurant for eating authentic South Indian food.

- For lunch, most of the people preferred Andhra style restaurants where lunch was served on banana leaves.

- A limited number of cities could be considered for such type of restaurants e.g. Bengaluru, Mysore and Mangalore (Karnataka), Hyderabad, Vijaywada and Vizag. (AP), Chennai, Madurai, Thiruchirapalli (TN) and Cochin and Thiruvanantapuram (Kerala).

- If Maharashtra is to be considered, it has more number of cities than the entire South India put together and in many cities, more than one such outlet could be setup.

- The per capita income of Maharashtra is better than South India and more number of outgoing people are available.

Will you help them decide by selecting an option for them and by giving reasons for the same?

Case Study - 9

INTERNATIONAL LEADS LTD.

With the advent of Internet marketing, getting contact details has become the biggest problem for most of the marketing companies. The contact details on the website are found to be old many times and not updated. So, sending e-mail on these e-mail addresses becomes futile as they all bounce back saying that they are not deliverable. Another problem that was faced by these marketing companies was that most of the websites gave contact details as info@xyz.com where xyz stood for the organization's name. These e-mail were filtered by the junior staff or staff of marketing and CRM departments and many times never reach the required senior person. Ashish Apte and Umesh Ranade looked at it as a big business opportunity and decided to start an organization by the name of 'International Leads Ltd.' They decided to do meta data farming in leads and sell them to clients at a price.

The modus operandi they thought was very simple, that could be listed as follows-

- Most of the employees had their e-mail addresses as follows: first name.lastname@companyname.com.

- The senior managers had their e-mail addresses as MD/COO/CEO@companyname.com.

- All senior managers were mostly listed on linkedin and their status was generally updated.

- By finding the names of senior people through linkedin and using the above formula, one could get the e-mail details of these persons.

- Telephone numbers of the organization were listed on the website.
- Personal phone numbers were available on linkedin.

Using this method, they started finding out the contact details of various organizations and advertised the service on their website and by using Internet marketing, reached many users for the same. Ashish and Umesh got very good response and many orders. They worked day and night and completed the orders and then went in for an office and a staff member who would do the work for them.

Since they did not want a continuous liability of many staff members, they were looking for persons with computer knowledge and willing to work for short periods at a low salary. They remembered their days while doing their MBA and the summer and winter project's work at no stipend or negligible stipend and thought of trying it out to get the students during the summer project. The idea clicked and many institutes were willing to send their students for the summer to them. So they selected four students each from five Institutes and arranged a place for them with laptops, in their office. All the students were promised incentives only if their contact details lead to closure (willing to meet the clients). There was no stipend for the work.

The students worked for eight weeks and developed around 1000 Indian and international contacts. All the students were given different countries and Indian states to find contacts. So within two months,20,000 international leads were collected which were authentic and reachable, at no cost at all. Those many leads, plus the contact details regularly generated by their own staff could take them through more than a year.

Questions

1. It is found that the most of web sites uploaded by many small and medium companies are not updated, is it done deliberately to avoid unnecessary traffic? Explain your answer.

2. Is it beneficial to use lead generating service or should the companies utilize their own staff for lead generation? Why?

Case Study - 10

HOSPITAL SERVICES

Dr. Gondhalekar was a successful second generation medical practitioner and a renowned surgeon. After working many years as an honorary surgeon at various city hospitals, he planned to open his own hospital. His family members supported him as many of his family members had also studied medicine and specialized in various fields of medicine. One of his cousins was an MD in Pathology and another was MS in Ophthalmology. Their family home which was commonly owned, was an old structure and many of the family members had shifted their residences to newer buildings in the vicinity.

They proposed to demolish the entire structure and rebuild a hospital in the place, but the family members did not agree on the financial matters and so it was decided to first start the hospital, see the progress and then decide on reconstruction. The hospital was started and since the old city area did not have any hospital in the vicinity, they started getting a steady stream of patients interested in eye surgery along with all sorts of pathological tests.

Once the hospital was accepted, the question of reconstruction of the building was sidelined. When the patients were accepting the service conditions there was no need to make new changes and waste money. Dr. Gondhalekar opened a clinic in the newer city area to catch patients from an affluent background. He started being present at the new clinic from 5pm to 6.30pm and accepted a maximum of 10 patients at the new clinic and then at the old place from 6.45pm to 8.30pm, taking in 18-20 patients. The system at the old place was that of enrolling your name during the day and coming at a given time, and at the new place, it was first come first serve basis (FCFS). The patients who could not manage to get an appointment at the old place would invariably go to the new place early, to get the appointment. Very few patients from an affluent background visited Dr. Gondhalekar's clinic, as better hospital facilities were available in newly developed areas.

The major problem with Dr. Gondhalekar's hospital was that there was no parking available. Additionally,, the old place was dingy, with lots of mosquitoes, but people staying in the same area were habituated to such conditions and felt nothing about it. The place was closer to their residences and they could walk to the hospital. Dr. Gondhalekar and his cousins put up a board in the waiting room that the consulting fees were voluntary and one could pay whatever they wanted to pay. This attracted many patients in the surrounding areas but the trick behind this was the pathology tests ordered were more than required and costing more than those in the other big hospitals. The surgical charges and nursing charges were also higher than big hospitals as the patients got more personalized care, but considering the dingy rooms, it was very high.

Dr. Gondhalekar's new clinic was well-decorated but the windows had no mosquito nets and no drinking water facility. People coming once would avoid coming the second time and they would ask Dr. Gondhalekar when he was available in the OPD of bigger hospitals. Dr. Gondhalekar, who was sitting in an A/C room never noticed the patients' inconvenience and when he was told about it, he ignored it. Many times, he would inform the receptionist that he was not coming and send all the emergency patients to the old clinic. Some patients then went to the old clinic and some would go to other surgeons.

A peculiar trend was observed by Dr. Gondhlekar. The patients from the new area would insist on getting operated in big hospitals on various pretexts like-

1. "Your old city hospital is far away and it will be inconvenient for family members to visit ."
2. "Parking is not available and my driver is on leave."
3. "We will get cashless facility at a bigger hospital, you don't give it etc."

Dr. Gondhalekar tried to tell these patients that he would not perform surgeries at bigger hospitals, as he needed to come many times, thus wasting his time. Some patients agreed to get operated at the old city hospital but many went and got themselves operated by other surgeons instead.

When Dr. Apterefered Mr. Nagarkar to Dr. Gondhalekar for getting operated for piles, he met him in the new area clinic and Dr. Gondhalekar asked him to do as many as 20 pathological tests at his hospital in the old area. The amount of mosquitoes in the clinic had annoyed Nagarkar a lot. Next day, Nagarkar went early morning without having even a drop of water and went through all the tests. He found that the staff was inefficient and no one was answerable to anyone. The tests were over by 9AM but he was asked to wait till Dr. Gondhalekar came. Nagarkar was worried about his car parked in front of a shop, as the old city area people were notorious for damaging vehicles for no reason whatever. The shopkeeper came at 9.30

PM and asked Nagarkar to move his car somewhere else. Somehow, he managed to park it about 100metres from the hospital, as the street vendors were expected after 10 am. Dr. Gondhalekar arrived at 10.30amand advised Mr. Nagarkar to collect the reports in the evening and get a fitness certificate from his family physician. Nagarkar couldn't fathom why this instruction was not given by any of the staff present.

Nagarkar had decided to get himself operated in a bigger hospital and told Dr. Gondhalekar about it. When Nagarkar was completing the formalities of cashless treatment, the clerk came and told him that Dr. Gondhalekar had refused to operate in that hospital, as the money offered by the hospital was less. Nagarkar asked her what her suggestion was. She said that he could get operated by another renowned surgeon available in the hospital. Nagarkar accepted the suggestion and got himself operated the next day, without informing Dr. Gondhalekar. He informed Dr. Apte that his friend was tricking the patients. On one side he was asking them to pay the visit fee voluntarily and then he was charging very high pathology and surgery charges. Nagarkar further said that he would get cured of piles but may contract dengue or chicken gunia in that hospital.

Questions

1. Will Dr. Aptegivea feedback to Dr. Gondhalekar?
2. Will Dr. Gondhalekar change his stance?
3. What actions would you suggest to Dr. Godhalekar for improving business?

CHAPTER 5

Cases in Agricultural Marketing

Case Study - 1

ONION FLAKES

Arivnd Deshpande, while doing a marketing project on the fluctuating prices of agricultural products, found that onion prices varied from Rs.10/- per kg to Rs.60/- per kg due to variations in the environmental conditions. The variations included-

1. High rains leading to loss of cultivation and price rise.
2. High yield without changes in demand, leading to drop in prices.
3. Lack of proper storage facility.
4. Low shelf-life of onions.

Fig. 5.1: Onion Flakes

Arvind also found that barring a few culinary dishes, onion was converted to pulp by cutting, frying and crushing it to improve the taste of the curry and the quantity of the curry. With some interaction with the women folk he found that in the earlier days when onions were not available the whole year round, housewives used to cut onions into flakes and dry them and store them for use, whenever needed. Arvind Deshpande also found that in Europe and USA, onion paste, onion flakes and onion powder was readily available in all the supermarkets, thus reducing the workload of the housewives.

The only problem was drying the onions which could not be done throughout the year. Even on sunny days it was time-consuming work and needed turning of the flakes to ensure uniform drying. To take care of this problem, he started looking for drier manufacturers. He had a choice of rotary driers and tray driers. Rotary driers had the following problems-

1. Constant speed needed to be maintained to ensure even and perfect drying. Maintaining the speed was a problem as the supply of electricity was constantly fluctuating.

2. The constantly fluctuating electric supply also made it difficult to maintain even temperature levels in the oven.

3. The staff required was more and needed to be efficient and alert or else the conveyor might move without the onions being loaded (automation is very expensive).

4. The conveyor needed to be cleaned regularly leading to stoppage of work.

The tray ovens were comparatively cheaper and took the same time to dry the onion flakes and gave the workers time to empty and fill the trays, if spare trays and tray trolleys were made available to them. Additional capacity generation was easier by adding new ovens in a row.

Arvind Deshpande decided to have his production unit outside Pune within a range of100kmsatShirur, where onion crop was easily available directly from the farmers, saving him transport cost and APMC charges and commissions.

He spoke to major retail chains and they showed interest in selling the onion flakes under their in-house brands. Arvind Deshpande also spoke to major restaurant owners, who showed interest in buying the onion flakes to save the cost of cooking.

The next problem was the storage of onions as the prices fluctuated quarterly (the crop comes in 100 days) and onions are available cheap when the crop comes out.

So he needed to make arrangements for the storage of onions for at least 120 days, (on the safer side). Onion storage is a tricky business; onion needs to be stored in a dry and airy place and many racks were needed to store onions in good condition.

He worked out the entire cost of the project and found that he was able to raise the same and decided to go ahead as good profits were assured.

Questions

1. What marketing opportunity do you see in this marketing environment?

2. What pricing policy will you use for your product?

Case Study - 2

PARESH BECOMES TECHNO-SAVVY

Paresh was a farmer in the backward area of Marathwada region of Maharashtra, with a very small land holding. He had taken education in agriculture and wanted to do farming. His land, though small, had various advantages like-

1. It had a well with year-round water.
2. It had a road connection with an internal farm road going beside his farm.
3. The land was plain and the soil was fertile.
4. It was at a lower level as compared to all the surrounding lands and held moisture for a longer time.

Paresh's father, Pandurang was a traditional farmer and grew only pulses in the kharip season and few vegetables for the rest of the year. Pandurang also planted some mango trees that yielded mangoes for their own consumption. Pandurang sold water from his well during the summer, which was used for drinking purpose by nearby villages. With all this, Pandurang managed to survive without the burden of any loan but was not a well-to-do farmer by any means. Paresh wanted to change this situation. He told his father that he wanted to look after the farm and that he wanted to change the farming pattern. His father readily agreed but said that getting farm laborers in other seasons except 'kharip' was difficult and costly, so he should plan his crop accordingly.

Paresh was not happy with the situation when he chanced to meet a field officer of a farming equipment manufacturer and talked to him about his problem. The field officer took him to their showroom and showed some of the farmers using their equipment and told him that if he was willing to use the farm equipment, he need not hire any labour. He also told him that the Government offered a high percentage of subsidy on farm equipment and banks gave loans readily. The field officer who was Paresh's senior in the Agriculture College took him to meet the field officer of another company selling fertilizers and insecticides. This other field officer suggested that Paresh go in for soyabean crop using farm equipment and take three crops per year, with the available well water. Paresh decided to become techno-savvy and plant the soyabean crop thrice a year in his land. He said to himself, "I want Good life so I must earn more from my farm."

Fig. 5.2: Techno-savvy

He went to the district place to find out what farm equipment was readily available so that it could be used to remove the necessity of farm labour. He also went to the rural development and agriculture support center to find what subsidies were available for farm equipment. He applied for the subsidy for drip irrigation equipment, rain sprinklers and a small multipurpose power tiller that could be used for ploughing, sowing and other functions. He went to the bank and applied for loans to buy all these equipment, so that he could have them in time after the 'Kharip' season was over.

Fig. 5.3: Farm Equipment

Pandurang was worried about the loans his son was taking and told Paresh that the loans could lead to disaster and suicide, as many farmers were doing, after being unable to repay the loans. Paresh said, "I am taking loans for farming unlike other farmers who take a crop loan from loan sharks for buying motorcycles and television sets. I will not take loans for such a purpose. I will buy my motorcycle and television set after I earn from farming. I want to construct our house first." Immediately after the 'Kharip' season was over, Paresh ploughed his land with the help of the power tiller and sowed soyabean again. He got the drip installed along with the rain sprinkler. He used proper fertilizers and insecticides by taking advice from the agriculture officers and had a bumper crop second time in the year. He did not stop there and went in for the third crop in the year, with the help of the well water and was able to clear most of the loans at the end of the year.

Paresh spoke to his uncle whose land was adjacent to his land but was at a higher level and was stony with no road connection, and asked him to sell the land to him. Paresh knew that with the water conservation techniques he was using, he could use the well water for a much bigger area and have a good yield. Paresh's uncle stayed in the city and his sons were not interested in farming and so they readily sold the land to Paresh. Next year, Paresh had double the land areas to till and make more profits. He first brought his uncle's plot to his level so that he could do the tilling of the larger plain plots effortlessly.

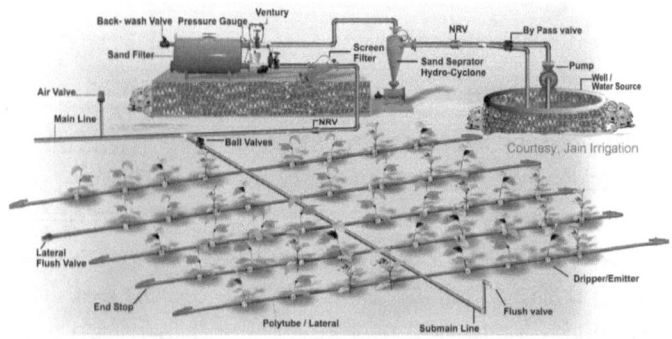

Fig. 5.4: Drip Irrigation System

Paresh was declared a "Pragatisheel farmer' and awarded a prize by the district collector at a function where Paresh told other farmers, "Become techno-savvy and save water to reap better rewards from farming." Paresh has now applied for a house building loan and hopes to go in for a large house that can give him the comforts of city life.

Questions

1. How did the equipment field officer convince Paresh to buy farm equipment and get his business?

2. How did the other field officer convince Paresh to go in for soyabean farming and get his business?

3. What problems were described by Pandurang?

4. How did Paresh overcome all the problems?

5. How could he manage to use well water for three crops?

Case Study - 3

GANESH GETS HIS BUSINESS

Ganesh joined MASF, a company renowned for its agricultural products for various crops, as a field officer. The company was supplying plant nourishment products that would lead to a higher yield and also specific insecticides that would take care of the plants against insect attacks which were common for that plant. Ganesh's basic education was B.Ag. and he had done MBA, Marketing from a reputed institute in Pune. After initial induction and on the job training, Ganesh was given charge of a newly created territory where the company's presence was negligible. Ganesh was given to understand that the organization knew that it was difficult to create their presence in the given area, as the competitor's product had ruled for a long time and its customers' loyalty was unshakable. But if Ganesh could establish the company presence, he would become an automatic choice for the post of Territory Manager in two years time, and would be entitled to the company- owned SUV for travel.

Fig. 5.5: Market

Ganesh started with farm visits early in the morning and surveyed the area growing tomato in each village, as he was planning to push the company's product specialized for tomato plants as tomato was a major crop in that area. While moving around he would talk to various farmers about the yield per acre and note it down in his diary. He found that the farmers were not being served by the rival company anymore as their market was fixed and they knew that the farmers would not move away easily from the trusted fertilizers, plant boosters and insecticides. The rival company kept the opinion leaders (mostly the sarpanch and other members of the village panchayat) happy by regularly using their farms as trial plots for various demonstrations and sometimes reimbursed them the demo expenditure without actually doing any demo. This kept the leaders happy and they promoted the rival company products regularly.

Ganesh arranged evening chawadi meetings for the farmers of various villages but was unable to attract a crowd. People were present at the spot but did not attend the meeting or listen to what he was saying. He was trying to get a sample plot for demo, but was still unable to get it even after establishing contacts with many farmers. Ganesh was disappointed because even at the end of three months he was unable to get a toe hold in the area. That month after his regional meeting he called his Marketing teacher and said that he wanted to discuss his career issues with him. He knew that his Marketing teacher took training programmes for various organizations. His Marketing professor agreed to meet him.

After listening to Ganesh's story the Marketing professor came out with the following questions-

1. Who are the opinion leaders? What castes do they belong to?
2. Do they get elected to the panchayat unopposed?
3. Have you found any personal rivalry between the groups in the villages?
4. Have you found anyone who has lost the panchayat election and has a grudge against the elected leaders?
5. Have you found any farmers who are willing to give land as a sample plot for demo but are not having quality land?

The Marketing professor then suggested to Ganesh that he should-

a. Look for such farmers who were getting low returns from their land and were not getting benefitted by the rival company and concentrate on them to get the sample plot.
b. Find out the rivalry between the groups and concentrate on the group that is being neglected by the rival company.
c. Befriend maximum persons in the villages, make a night halt at some villages and spend money on these friends in the villages.
d. Run a quiz contest based on the information from presentations and at the end of the presentations, reward people who give the right answers.
e. Arrange some kind of product exhibition for the farmers in a few villages and serve snacks to farmers who attend it.

The Professor said, "Try these ideas and come back to me after three months to give me a report."

Ganesh prepared proposals for the quiz contest and exhibition and got it sanctioned from his regional manager and then started having evening *Chawadi* meetings. The rewards attracted the attention of the farmers and they started listening to what Ganesh was saying and even came forward to give sample plots. The caste equation helped and some lower caste farmers gave him plots for sample and because the yields were good, they started buying his product. At the end of the third month, Ganesh called his Professor and said that he was unable to meet him personally but the plan was working and he would come with the actual results in another month's time.

At the end of six months, at the meeting in the regional office, his RSM spoke good about him and said that the results were encouraging and soon they would have a strong presence in the new area. At the end of the year, Ganesh had established a strong presence in the area with more than 25% market share. He was happy and confident of becoming a Territory Manager at the end of the second year in the company.

Questions

1. What procedure did Ganesh use to contact the farmers initially?
2. What strategy did Ganesh's professor suggest to him?
3. What is the learning from this case?

Case Study - 4

EARN MORE MONEY

Yogesh Chavan, an Agriculture graduate completed his MBA in Marketing. Born and brought up in Pune district, he wanted to work for an Agri-Business company in Pune district only. Mr. Sarker, the Regional Manager in an Agri-Business MNC had visited Yogesh's institute and had given a lecture on how joining the Marketing Department of an Agri-Business company was good and had many opportunities. Yogesh met Mr. Sarker and asked him to help him a get job in Agri-Business marketing and if possible, in the organization where he was working. Mr. Sarker said that a few vacancies were coming up, mostly in the floral division that was being set up by their company but there would be lot of hard work as the company was entering the market which was dominated by others. Yogesh said that he would wait and was willing to work hard and ensure that his recruitment was worthwhile.

When Yogesh joined, he was initially trained in Pune district where he learned the procedures of selling and convincing the customers of company products, for growing tomato. Afterwards, he was sent for training to another state, where the company's floral business was established, so that he could get confidence in the company products. Yogesh had the opportunity to meet various farmers who had gained and made money out of the flower export business, even though they had smaller plots.

Yogesh came back confident enough to achieve the company targets for the district, as he was alone in the district from the flower division. He started with his native village in Junnar tehsil as most of the land was irrigated there and very fertile. The climate in Pune district was supportive of the flower business and export facility of flowers was also available at Pune airport.

Yogesh started meeting various farmers and asking them-

1. What crop they took?
2. How many times they took a crop in a year?
3. What was the per acre yield?
4. At what rate they sold their yield?
5. What were the net earnings from the crop per acre per year?
6. Would they be interested in changing the crop for better earning?

Yogesh was disappointed by the farmers' responses. Most of the farmers were conservative and not willing to change the crop pattern. Many followed the village elders, even when they were not making enough money. Most of them were afraid of change as they did not want to venture into unknown zones, even when the prospects were good. Everyone was willing to follow the successful leader, but not interested in becoming a pioneer. Yogesh was worried and he could see his failure, if he was unable to get any results at the end of the first quarter of the year. His manager said that he didn't expect any positive results in the first quarter but at least the progress had to look positive.

Yogesh started revising his notes given by his Marketing professor and found the following tips very useful for getting started. The tips were as follows-

a. No one buys without a valid need, except for fashionable goods.

b. If there is no need, a sales person should create a situation where the customer feels the need.

c. Createa desire to buy the product through effective brand talk developed through FAB (features, advantages and benefits) analysis.

d. Ensure satisfaction of the customer to get mouth publicity.

e. Do not forget the AIDAS formula of sale (attention, interest, desire, action and satisfaction).

So Yogesh decided to find a farmer who had a valid reason to shift to a new crop pattern. He found a farmer called Yeshwant with a small farm holding normally growing sugarcane for jaggery-making. That year the Government had banned jaggery-making in the area and he had been unable to sell his sugarcane to jaggery-makers. Since he was not a member of any sugar factory, they refused to buy his sugarcane ahead of the members. Yeshwant somehow managed to sell his sugarcane to the sugarcane juice makers but could earn nothing out of it. He was looking for a change in crop and Yogesh met him at the right time. So Yogesh was happy to clear his first hurdle -he had found a person with a genuine need.

Yeshwant was sceptical about the expenditure on the flower business as it needed a greenhouse and other infrastructural investments. If the venture failed then the infrastructure created would have gone waste. Yogesh promised Yeshwant that the greenhouse would lead to high returns and the choice of more varieties of flowers could be grown after the first season of 100 days had passed and he would be confident of high returns.

He suggested that Yeshwant should go in for only roses and gladiolas to begin with, and once he was convinced and confident he could erect a greenhouse and go in for different varieties that could even be sold domestically. Ganesh took Yeshwant to an exporter of flowers who promised good rates if the quality was as per the requirement of international customers. Yeshwant accepted but said that Yogesh's company should use his farm as a sample plot and spend the initial money.

FLOWERING PLANTS

Fig. 5.6: Flowering Plant Crop

Yogesh talked to his Regional Manager, Mr. Sarkar who readily accepted as it was an entry in the area. Yogesh remembered that he must try and get the maximum attention of the other farmers when Yeshwant's farm was being used as a sample plot. So when he could get the farm ploughed and the seeds were sowed and drip irrigation system was in place, he put up notice boards at prime locations in the village (panchayat house, temples etc.) and advised farmers to come and visit the Yeshwant's farm at a particular time to get more information about flowers as crops. Yogesh carried a portable LCD projector along with his laptop and showed the farmers' films on flower crops shot in other locations and testimonials of farmers from other regions. Fortunately the climatic conditions remained good and the first lot of gladiolas was ready for shipment. Yeshwant got handsome returns and immediately went in for a greenhouse that helped him go for another season. Yeshwant earned more than his earnings from sugarcane in the first two seasons itself and the third season was the bonus.

Yogesh took videos of Yeshwant's farms and his testimonial which he showed to other farmers and thus, he got some more farmers to change over to flower farming. The farmers made money and Yogesh also got praise from his superiors and good incentives for his efforts.

Yogesh was of the opinion that now his company should appoint one more field officer to promote the flower business, as the area given to him was very large. Since the initial ground work was already done by him, the momentum should not be lost.

Questions

1. What strategy did Yogesh use for getting the farmers to enter the flower business?

2. What would you do in Yogesh's place in similar situations?

3. Should Mr. Sarkar, the RM go in for additional field officers for the district?

Case Study - 5

VEGETABLE HOME DELIVERY

Nilesh Pawar was from the farming community and was interested in doing business related to agricultural products. He did his MBA in Marketing and was much interested in the subject of entrepreneurship development. After completing his MBA, he told his father that he would like to start the business of selling vegetables from his farm directly to the customers, without going through middlemen who make more money than the farmers. His father said, "Your idea is good but the Government rules prohibit us from selling our produce directly to the end customers. We must go through the APMC (Agro Produce Marketing Committee) and accept whatever rate they give us.

Nilesh went and saw the method of auction that took place in APMC. There was no transparency in it, and the registered commission agents (a date – auctioning agents who operate on 2.5% commission) were only authorized to conduct auctions and they were not openly called for. Two people came ahead, shook hands and placed a handkerchief on their hands and made some movements of the fingers and the rate was declared. No one knew what was decided, why it was decided, how it was decided and why others were not allowed to openly give their offers. The registered commission agents took their commission for not doing anything in favour of the farmers. Another thing was that smaller lots were not auctioned at all and were mixed with other lots, even when the quality differed.

Fig. 5.7: Vegetable Home Delivery

Nilesh did not like the system and started thinking of a via media for his business. He clearly saw that if his vegetables were offered at Rs.10/ kg, they were being sold in retail for Rs.40 as the retailers purchased it from the commission agents for Rs.30/kg. The commission agents were earning Rs.20/kg for doing nothing and the farmer and the customers were at a loss as they were paying more money unnecessarily. He found that if he sold his vegetables after cleaning and cutting them in pieces (for cooking) and kept them in packets, they were treated as processed vegetables and could be sold directly without going through the APMC.

Nilesh started with one of the middle and upper income group residential areas and collected the following information-

1. What was their daily quantity of consumption of vegetables?

2. What were their favorite vegetables?

3. Did they repeat the same vegetables in a week?

4. Did they cook vegetables in the morning and in the evening?

5. How many persons were there in their family?

6. Did they mix vegetables while cooking? If yes, what were the combinations and in what proportion?

7. What herbs were used along with the vegetables?

8. What was the amount of tomatoes used along with which vegetables?

9. How many times did they use leafy vegetables? If they were using them less number of times, was it because it required a lot of time for cleaning and cutting?

10. If leafy vegetables were supplied after cleaning and cutting would they like to have them every week?

After getting these answers, he made a weekly plan for customers purchasing vegetables once in a day for morning use and twice a day for both time cooking. A third plan was made for people who cooked two vegetables every time. He made enough copies of these plans and fixed a monthly rate that showed the price of vegetables plus service charges of cleaning cutting and home delivery. And he started collecting orders with 50% advance. He got many interested customers and saw that some customers were willing but hesitated to give him advance. He knew they would join the next month. The price was equivalent to the average retail price of vegetables. Nilesh knew that he was going to earn a good profit as the cost of vegetables (from his and his neighbour's farms) was very low.

He gave the same plan to his father and installed machinery for cleaning and dicing the vegetables. He also explained to his mother what quantities and ingredients needed to be packed together and how the packets needed to be sealed.

He started earning good profits from the first month itself and employed people to help him and his family members for cleaning, packaging and delivery.

Nilesh said to himself, "Even if the rules of APMC change, I don't care now that I have my business of farming and selling farm produce at a profit."

Questions

1. Do you think the APMC system is beneficial for farmers? Give reasons

2. The current system of reaching the city customers through APMC helps only the middlemen, do you agree this statement? Give reasons

3. How will customer get vegetables and fruits in reasonable rates while farmers get good returns? Explain in detail

CHAPTER 6

Cases in Rural Marketing

Case Study - 1

NIRMA BECOMES THE NO.1 BRAND

Nirma–washing powder was launched in Nadiad, a town in Gujarat way back in the 60s. Gujarat is a very price-sensitive market. The product was well accepted in Gujarat. In the late 70's when the brand was launched in Mumbai, it had a mixed response. It was getting good response in the price-sensitive markets in Mumbai like Mulund, Ghatkopar, Dharavi, Malad, Borivli etc. The brand also had a good response in the lower income areas of Parel, Lalbaug, Vikhroli, Deonar etc. In other areas, the product was not well-accepted.

The product had the following competitors-

1. 'Surf' at the higher end (a detergent and not a washing powder)

2. 'Key' detergent powder at the middle range (again a detergent and not a washing powder)

3. Local brands of soap flakes.

Since the middle and upper class consumers had upgraded themselves from washing powders and soap flakes, they were not expected to come back to it again. To gain volumes, Nilima needed regular consumers and not the lower income group consumers who could not form a core group (they could not be expected to be brand-loyal).

Nirma did some consumer and market research which brought in the following facts-

1. HLL was present only in the urban and semi-urban markets.

2. HLL had skeletal service in some rural markets, where it was sold against cash and the service was not regular, thus increasing the investment of rural dealers.

3. Godrej Soaps was totally absent in the semi-urban and rural markets.

4. Swastik, another major brand from the Sarabhai's was not available in the rural markets as it was selling all their own products and products of Beecham India (Brylcream, Maclean's tooth paste and ENO) in urban markets, through their marketing subsidiary, HPMA (Home Products Marketing Agency).

5. There were no branded washing powders available in the rural markets.

6. The thought behind it was that consumers in the rural market used washing soaps of cheap quality and no one bothered to soak the clothes in soap/detergent powder before washing.

7. The washing soaps like BB, WW were hot favorites of all the rural consumers.

8. Soap flakes were being used to some extent by the educated middle income group customers, but these soap flakes took a longer time to dissolve and needed hot water for doing so.

9. There was a big opportunity in the rural markets only if the rural consumers were explained the benefits of using detergent powder.

10. There should be a way to sell the products at affordable rates, even after taking into consideration the high cost of rural marketing.

Nirma went in for a specialized rural marketing plan. They appointed super distributors for each district. These super distributors were required to sell in both urban, semi-urban and rural markets on a fixed frequency. Nirma subsidized the van and the salesman's expenses. Nirma was heavily advertised on electronic media. Their promotional team demonstrated how the use of detergent powder reduces efforts in washing clothes and requires lesser water, as it requires rinsing of washed clothes less number of times. To control the cost of production, more number of production units were established below the threshold limit of getting in the excise duty bracket, saving a good amount of the 15% cost that goes as excise duty.

All these things lead to establishing the brand strongly in the rural market. The consumers in the rural markets got a brand that was famous and gave them a guarantee of 'SAFEDI' at a low cost. There were no strong contenders and Nirma could establish itself without any problem.

Since the rural market was much bigger in size than the urban market, Nirma became the No.1 brand (volume sales) in India in a short span of time.

HLL had to come up with new brands through a separately established subsidiary (Wheel, Sunlight) to dislodge Nirma and took more than 10 years to do so.

Questions

1. What strategy did Nirma use to capture market share? Was it right? Why/

2. With 60% population staying in rural areas why rural markets are still neglected by major brands?

3. To improve conditions of rural marketing what facilities are needed for the marketing companies?

Case Study - 2

CROWN GOES RURAL

Crown Bakery which started in the 1960s as a small bakery producing bread in different sizes in Kanpur, slowly graduated to manufacturing of cream biscuits, rusks and cookies of various types. In the late 1980s, they put up an automatic biscuit making plant along with a franchisee for a bread-making company to produce and distribute sliced packaged bread for them. The spare capacity of bread was also used for making bread in their name and was branded as 'CROWN' They had also opened 10 shops in Kanpur for selling their products. To utilize the spare capacity of biscuit-making, they explored the markets of Lucknow, Allahabad and Banaras. The products were then sold in other cities throughout UP and so, Crown Bakery increased their production capacity.

Fig. 6.1: Crown Goes Rural

In the new millennium, Indian markets were opened for international brands which were very aggressive in their promotional activities and had better packaging and varieties. They started eating into the market share of Crown. The marketing team of Crown became worried about their future, and many of the Crown sales staff with better educational qualifications joined the MNC biscuit makers for better prospects. The owner of Crown Bakery, Sohrab Mehta called for a meeting of the sales managers and asked them to come out with good suggestions that could be implemented to get a hold on the sales volumes and growth.

During the meeting most of the sales managers came out with similar suggestions like-

1. Reduce the price tag to 10% lower than the MNC products.
2. Open up states like Bihar, Jharkhand, Madhya Pradesh to get additional sales volumes.
3. Start selling in Delhi.
4. Advertise on television channels.
5. Give promotions to the tradesmen as well as consumers etc.

When Sohrab asked them for chances of success, most of them said, "We must try our best and accept the results as they come."

Mr. Rakesh Nigam, the Sales Manager looking after Allahabad came out with different suggestions. He suggested the following and said that this would give 100% positive results. The suggestions were-

1. Increase the price tag to MNC product levels.
2. Improve packaging to make it more attractive and increase the shelf life.
3. Come out with smaller packets.

4. Use local channels to promote the product, especially the cable network that is much cheaper and can be focused.

5. Appoint distributors in smaller towns and give them van allowance to cover nearby villages on a fixed coverage plan basis.

6. Give them target-based incentives and extend the incentives to the van sales team (salesman, driver and loader).

7. Use OOH (out of home) publicity in the rural market especially wall paintings, and name boards for rural restaurants and canteens.

8. Give dispensers to rural retailers, restaurants and canteens buying pre-decided quantities.

9. Announce an incentive scheme for company sales officers and managers recruiting a maximum number of rural distributors that work for at least six months in a row.

Sohrab was impressed with Nigam's proposal and asked him to stay back and work out the details of initial expenditure, price lists and promotional expenditure. The figures worked by Nigam along with the factory staff and Finance Manager looked very impressive. Sohrab was wondering whether he should go ahead and implement the proposal.

Questions

1. Should Sohrab accept the proposal? Give reasons.

2. Why was Nigam asking for cable TV and OOH publicity instead of TV channels?

Case Study - 3

ASHOK DEVELOPS THE RURAL MARKET

Ashok joined SFPL (Shrirang Food Products Ltd.) producing various products like pickles, Hakka noodles, pasta in various forms, semolina, ginger paste, garlic paste, black pepper powder, table salt, and some condiments and ready–to-cook mixes. SFPL was a new startup company and it was trying to set up itself in the market. The company was started by Mrs. Kulkarni after her son Shriranggot a degree in Food Technology. Mrs. Kulkarni used to make various condiments and sold them from house to house and had some retailers who kept her products and sold them regularly for commission. Her business was set for a particular quantity and her son wanted to increase the scope of business by going in for brand value, with products being sold in attractive packs. Mrs. Kulkarni had procured a plot in MIDC and had started producing some of her products on a larger scale and packing them in their own brand. So what she had to do was add packaging machines to her set-up and start selling the products in her own brand also. Shrirang added some refining to her products to make them last longer as they were packaged commodities. He also added some new products like ready mixes, semolina, pasta and products like ginger-garlic paste, mayonnaise, mustard paste etc.

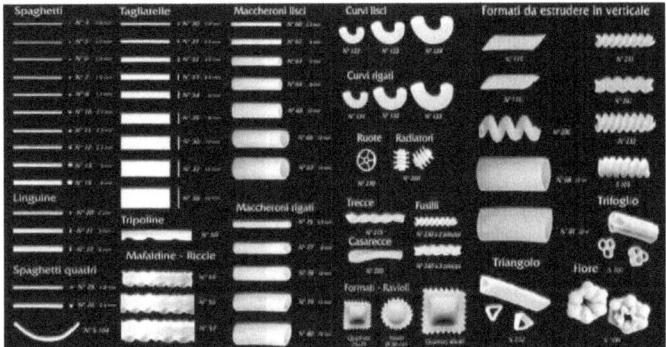

Fig. 6.2: Ashok Develops the Rural Market

Shrirang was required to visit various retailers and persuade them to stock and sell the SFPL products and was not in a position to immediately appoint a large number of sales staff and advertise the products. Looking after the production and also sales was becoming difficult for Shrirang, but no distributors were willing to accept an agency and the people who were ready asked for long credit periods and high margins, that were impossible for Shrirang. Shrirang consulted his Uncle who was working as a Sales Manager in some FMCG company and asked him for guidance. His uncle gave him the following suggestions-

1. Appoint a sales person on salary plus commission basis where the salary quotient would be low and incentives would be high.

2. The incentives would be payable after the recovery of payment of goods sold, and in proportion to the payment received.

3. No expired goods would be accepted back (shelf life of the products was 6 to 12 months).

4. The salesman was free to sell products anywhere with no area limitations.

5. If the salesman succeeded in appointing a distributor who worked for at least 6 months continuously, a separate incentive of 1% of total purchases (product delivered and payments received) made by the distributor would be paid to the salesman.

Shrirang liked the idea and gave advertisements in the classified column in local newspapers for walk-in interviews. Not many responses were received for the classified advertisements but Shrirang was able to shortlist two persons among them. One of them was having two years' work experience but was asking for a high salary and low incentive structure and another was Ashok, with no field experience but who had worked as a stall salesman in exhibitions during his vacations and was willing to take a low salary and high incentives, provided his mobile bill and petrol expenses were paid separately. Shrirang agreed to his demand and fixed a daily petrol allowance based on the average expected travel per day.

Ashok who came from a lower middle class family and needed the job urgently, started working immediately. Ashok had come across a book in Marathi called 'Adarsh Vikreta' which explained many tricks for selling FMCG products and he had liked it. Some of the points from the book that he liked were-

1. A sale is not complete unless money is recovered.
2. Both, the buyer and seller must be satisfied with the sale.
3. MORE customers buying MORE quantity, MORE number of times leads to higher and higher sales.

4. When competition is present, QPS superiority helps i.e. either your QUALITY or PRICE or SERVICE must be superior to your competitors.

Ashok thought of using these principles to get MORE customers buying MORE quantity, MORE number of times. He started calling on the maximum number of retailers every day. Many times he used to end up meeting more than 150 retailers in a day. To ensure that he visited all the available retailers, he divided the city into twelve zones, so that he could visit all the retailers in two weeks and start repeat visits afterwards. He started carrying products along with him so that he could give ready delivery and avoided orders getting cancelled. This paid rich dividends as Ashok sold everything against cash and only small quantities per retailer. He was thus able to sell the entire quantity he carried with him. In a few days he came to know what products were more acceptable when pushed, and started carrying them in more quantity.

Within three months, SFPL's sale had more than doubled and so Ashok was able to get a reasonable monthly income. Shrirang also increased his salary quotient and gave him a certificate of good work to boost his morale. One day after working in a particularly faraway area of the city and not getting good business, Ashok strayed in a village outside the city limits. He found that because that area was not being serviced by most of the organizations, he received a good response and all his stock of products was sold out in just a few outlets. He visited other outlets and collected orders to be delivered the next day. The next day he started early in the morning with the stock for supply against the orders he had taken, plus additional quantities for visiting more outlets or visiting outlets in the city area while returning home. He was able to sell all the quantity he had carried and recovered all the money. When he talked to the retailers they told him that the next day was the Weekly Bazaar day and many villagers from the nearby smaller villages visited the place. Since TV advertisements were being aired for various products, the consumers demanded them and were not particular about the brand. If the packing was attractive, they readily bought any brand. They requested Ashok to come every week on that day so that they could buy the required quantity; they also said that the other companies visited them once a month and insisted on them buying larger quantities. Ashok agreed and decided to do so.

After returning home, Ashok sat with the map of the city and found all the surrounding villages and their bazaar days. He reworked his city visit plans in such a way that he could spare a few days a week to visit these villages. He found that there were a number of potential villages for which he could not spare time. So he thought of appointing a distributor for the city area, who could cover the major areas every week and Ashok could have spare time. As the business of SFPL had stabilized, there were a few distributors willing to work on company terms. So Ashok had discussions with Shrirangand Shrirang promised incentives to Ashok on the sales done by the distributors and also that he would increase his petrol allowance to take care of his visits to the villages. Ashok started visiting the surrounding villages and gota good amount of business and also good salary and incentives. After a period of time, Shrirang decided to appoint another salesman with Ashok as the supervisor and fixed incentives for Ashok. Incidentally, the new salesman was the same person who had been short listed along with Ashok but had refused the job!

Questions

1. What was the selling policy adopted by Ashok initially?

2. Why was Ashok able to get good business from the outskirts of the city?

3. What lessons should a marketing person take from this case study?

Case Study - 4

SUCCESS THROUGH SATELLITE DISTRIBUTION

'Pass-hamesha' a brand of mobile instrument was contract manufactured in China for an Indian company and sold all over India through normal marketing channels of franchisee outlets being supplied by depots in all the states. The basic USPs for 'Pass-hamesha' were-

1. Sturdy body.
2. Longer battery life.
3. Solar battery charging.
4. Many languages for sending SMS.
5. FM/SW radio.
6. Music storage.
7. 7.4 pixel camera.
8. Multimedia.
9. Low-priced.
10. Android system (smart phone).

Because of all these features, its body was a little heavy and was not sleek and also not very attractive to look at. The company targeted only the lower end of the market and had limited success and steady sales. The company was not very happy with the volume of business and the manufacturer in China wanted them to buy higher quantities or give them an upward rate revision of 10%.

A new sales manager, Manoj Gawade, an MBA in Marketing from a reputed institute who had worked in the FMCG sector with expertise in rural marketing came up with the idea of selling the product in the rural market. Historically, the company had failed to get franchisee outlets in smaller towns as they were unable to purchase the minimum stipulated quantity at a time and servicing these franchisees was not cost-effective, without their purchasing the minimum stipulated quantity regularly.

Manoj Gawade did a quick survey of a few rural markets and came up with the following proposal of selling through satellite (Hub and Spoke) distribution strategy for the rural markets -

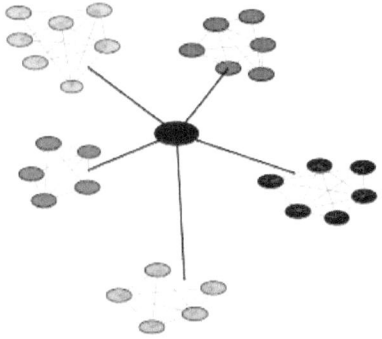

Fig. 6.3: Hub & Spoke Distribution System

1. Appointing a franchisee at every tehsil place/town with a population of over 20,000.

2. He should be motivated/helped to appoint sub-franchisees at small town's/villages in the periphery, parting with his margin.

3. These sub-franchisees would sell products in their area.

4. The main franchisee would get a separate bonus for the sale he had done to the sub-franchisee (bills to be submitted in support).

5. Main franchisees to get a target bonus in slabs where a high bonus would be available at a higher level of achievements.

6. The additional cost of reward bonuses would cost the company a maximum of 5% of the additional sales generated, so the total additional cost was expected to be less than 2% on total sales.

The company directors had gone through the proposal and were discussing whether to accept the proposal or reject it. Help them decide on the proposal.

Questions

1. What are the benefits of satellite (axis and spokes) marketing? Can it be used for all type of products? Explain how.

2. What are the major problems in rural marketing? How can they be eliminated?

CHAPTER 7

<hr>

Cases in Consumer Behaviour

Case Study - 1

BELIEFS AND ATTITUDES TOWARDS FOOD

Madhavrao was a well-to-do, hardworking businessman. He was able to buy a small independent house for himself and was staying with his family. He was very proud of his family heritage and strictly followed the culture set by his forefathers. He and his family were strictly vegetarians and would buy food articles only from reputed dealers for purity. He had one buffalo at his house and all the members of his family had a healthy habit of consuming milk and milk products made from the milk of this buffalo. Madhavrao had three coconut trees and his family liked to add fresh coconut to all the food recipes. His family always used fresh ground nut oil for cooking and was fond of home-made pickles, papad etc. Madhavrao had joined a sports club and used to play tennis twice a week to keep fit. He was hale and hearty and enjoyed his life.

One day Madhavrao felt giddiness and chest pain, and he thought that something must be wrong in his food the previous day so he did 'Langhan' (had no food) that day to give rest to his system. He was okay the next day. The giddiness became a regular occurrence which Madhavrao ignored and one fine day he had a massive heart attack. After angiography he was diagnosed to have four blockages that required immediate bypass operation.

The operation went well and when the heart specialist asked Madhavrao to change his food habits, Madhavrao was surprised. "But this is the food my father and my father's father used to eat and they had no problems of cholesterol or hypertension!" The doctor said "Those days were different. People used to walk a lot and burn all the calories they consumed. Besides, how do you know whether they had this problem or not? Both of them died in their early 60's. Today's life is faster and leads to a lot of frustration which leads to tensions. In addition, the unburnt calories that you accumulate through eating coconut and ghee lead to building of high cholesterol levels in your blood. The high amount of salt through pickles and papad helps the cholesterol block the blood vessels and so there is high blood pressure.

The doctor said, "No more coconut in all food preparations, no more pickles and papads, cut down on salt and ghee and start using refined sunflower oil."

Madhavrao said, "I always believed that my food habits were the most healthy food habits as I followed my forefathers. I am proved wrong."

Questions

1. What was wrong with Madhavrao's habits? Why were the habits that were good for his   forefathers wrong for his generation?

2. How will you take advantage of the situation to sell food products containing low cholesterol?

Case Study - 2

SWAMIJI REFUSES FOOD AT SADASHIVRAO'S HOUSE

Sadashivrao was happy that Swamiji had agreed to come to his house and have some snacks. Swamiji had planned to come on a Monday with his followers and all of them observed fast on that day. While Swamiji only took milk and some fruits on Monday, his followers took light snack food that was allowed on a fasting day.

Sadashivrao made lavish arrangements for the occasion and had ordered the cook to make Sabudana wada, sabudana khichadi and sabudana thalipeeth along with fruits, flavoured sweet milk and lassi.

Swamiji came at the appointed hour with his entourage. After the padya-pooja, Sadashivrao offered fruits and plain milk to Swamiji and the other snacks to his followers. His followers refused to take the snacks sighting Swamiji's orders for not having food of foreign origin on the day of the fast. Sadashivrao was very sad and asked them, "But this is the normal food everyone has on the day of fasting, even on Ekadashi and Sankashti Chaturthi?" The followers said, "Ask Swamiji and he will give a proper explanation." Swamiji explained as follows-

1. Sabudana is made from tapioca root which is not of Indian origin. It was brought to India by the European rulers. Secondly, while making sabudana, it is decolorized by using animal bones.

2. Potato is also not of Indian origin. It came to India with the Europeans as it was their staple food.

3. The chillies used for making the food spicy are also not of Indian origin. Ancient Indians used black pepper and not chillies.

4. Sugar is only allowed when it is hand-made - that is 'khandsari' or else jaggery should be used for sweetening. Sugar from factories is not allowed as the whitening process is similar to that of sabudana.

Sadashivrao ordered more fruits and offered only fruits to the followers of Swamiji. He said to himself, "And I thought I was right all these days."

Questions

1. What must be the reason behind the acceptance of sabudana, potato and sugar as food acceptable on the fasting day?

2. Will this knowledge of sabudana, potato and chillies being of foreign origin make any difference to people's habits?

Case Study - 3

REJECTION OF INDIAN BRANDS

Prakash Bandal passed out of a management institute and joined an Indian laptop manufacturer as a Business Development Officer (BDO). His institute was providing branded laptops of an international company to all the students. His batch had received laptops of a particular international brand which was not the same as the laptop of the international brand received by his previous batch students, because they faced many problems in that brand. As his batch also encountered many problems with the laptops, starting from late delivery (the term started in July and they got laptops in next January) to battery and the LCD screen not functioning properly etc. and so the next batch received laptops of another international brand.

As he had seen three different international brands not giving satisfaction to the customers (students), he was very confident that he would be able to push the Indian brand of laptops that was being offered at a much lesser price and longer warranty period.

He called on many management institutes and submitted his quotation. He was short listed for giving the order but was not given the order and the orders went to international brands which had quoted rates higher than his by more than Rs.2000/-. He was unable to understand the reason. Even the institute where he studied did not give him the order and the order went to the same international brand that had defaulted earlier.

He went and talked to the Chairman of the institute and he got his answer. The Chairman said, "Our promotional brochure says laptops of reputed brand. Your brand is not reputed as it is new and Indian." He went and met the Director and said, "Why can you not accept an Indian brand as reputed?" The Director said, "Sorry I cannot change the attitude of the people towards Indian brands."

Questions

1. What should be Prakash Bandal's line of action to overcome this obstacle?

2. What do you think is the reason behind people's attitude towards Indian brands?

Case Study - 4

UNDERSTAND CONSUMER'S NEED TO GET BUSINESS - THE ASIAD STORY

Till the end of 1982, commuters between Mumbai and Pune had the following choices:

1. Use of Railway—Less frequency required, one week advance booking, time taken- 4 hours

2. Useof ST—Less frequency, uncomfortable, took at least 5 hours.

3. Useof taxi – Faster service, took 3.5 hours, would start after getting 4 passengers, charges were 5 times that of ST and 7 times that of railway. During season, the availability was poor.

There was a clear-cut need for a faster cost-effective and timely service which was comfortable also.

Fig. 7.1: Asian Games 1982- State Govt. supplied buses that were used afterwards as ASIAD Buses

During 1982,the Government of India asked the State Transports to buy 20 buses and loan them to the

Government for using them at the time of the Asian Games. After the Asian Games, these buses were to be used for normal use. All these buses were fitted with comfortable seats. Most of the states used them as luxury buses on various routes. State Transport of Maharashtra planned a different use. They announced a timely (every half hour frequency) luxury bus service between Mumbai and Pune, starting from a special bus stand called ASIAD stand (the buses had the Asian Games logo painted on it) which was opposite the Mumbai Pune taxi service stand.

The following points were covered-

1. Timely service – The frequency of the bus was maintained every 30 minutes even if the bus was empty.

2. Comfort – More leg space than taxi and better seats.

3. Cheaper service – Rs.60 per person as against Rs. 180 per seat of taxi.

4. Faster service – Maximum time declared to be 4 hours for reaching the destination.

5. Extra buses, if required, based on the number of passengers standing in queue.

MSRTC had done its homework properly. They had their media communication also clearly stating the plus points. They had a winning formula. The service was declared to be a hit and proved to be a money spinner for MSRTC. Following effects were noticed-

1. The taxi service was badly hit. The drivers doing at least 2 trips every day started doing 2 trips every week.

2. Normal Mumbai-Pune buses started running empty. MSRTC had to cancel them.

3. Railway traffic was affected. Trains became less crowded.

4. Many company executives travelling in company cars started preferring ASIADs to company cars (cost-saving plus more comfort).

All this was done by people managing a PSU (Public Sector Unit) owned by the Government of Maharashtra. MSRTC earned profits and was the only SRTC to be profitable in India.

One must say, "Find an opportunity through understanding the consumer need and you have a big business at hand."

Questions

1. What were the consumer needs for Mumbai-Pune travel?

2. What was the USP of the Asiad buses?

3. What lessons one can learn out of this study?

Note: Selfish politicians then permitted private tour operators to run point-to-point bus services with no levies and burdens that are paid by MSRTC like-

1. Infrastructure development surcharge.

2. Education cess.

3. Passenger tax.

4. Free travel to freedom fighters.

5. Student concessional passes.

6. Senior citizen concessions.

7. Minimum service to uneconomical routes.

8. Not allowing commercially developed bus stands.

9. Allowing maxi-cabs on all routes.

10. Low controlled fares.

Currently MSRTC is loss-making and the Government owes it a lot of funds.

Case Study - 5

THE AUTOMOBILE SHOWROOM CASE

Patil Automobiles was a reputed automobile showroom in Pune working for a reputed company selling LCVs and cars. It was centrally located and had a very large area to take care of the showroom and service station needs. The popular brand had only one such showroom and service station in the city and the district.

Since the company had only one such showroom, the workers at Patil Automobiles had become arrogant and careless. They would force the consumers to replace parts which did not require replacement. The reason behind this was that the workers were paid commissions on the bill of the customer and they used to inflate the customer's bill to earn the commission.

The situation changed once the automobile company appointed additional dealers in the city and the district. While the sale at Patil Automobiles dropped marginally, the business at the service station dropped heavily.

While customers got their free servicing done at Patil Automobiles, the subsequent servicing was done at other service stations. The older customers also stopped coming to Patil Automobiles and started getting their vehicles serviced at the new service stations.

The owners of Patil Automobiles were worried. For automobile showrooms, the spares business is a long-term business and a more profitable one. The spares and service business was dropping. They contacted a management college to do a consumer satisfaction survey to find out the reasons for the drop. The survey showed the following-

1. The showroom salesmen were very good and of a helping nature.

2. The loans were arranged very fast.

3. The vehicle delivery was very fast.

4. The RTO registration was done fast and the customers got the registration number that they wanted at a low cost.

5. The service station workers were rude.

6. The service station workers didn't care for the customer's urgency.

7. The service station delayed the servicing.

8. The vehicle was out of work for at least two to three days.

9. The delivery was not timely. They would call at a given time and then say that the vehicle was not ready and hence ask the customer to come the next day.

10. The bill was always high.

11. The parts were changed unnecessarily.

12. Servicing at other service stations took half the time and the costs were one-third of that of Patil Automobiles.

The owners of Patil Automobiles were shocked to read the report. They later on ran a campaign to change the image of the service station by calling all the lapsed customers and inviting them to get their vehicles serviced at Patil Automobiles again. This shows that-

"Consumer satisfaction is a must in the competitive environment."

Questions

1. What went wrong in the Patil Automobile business?

2. How can one ensure customer satisfaction in such a business?

3. As the owner of an Automobile showroom and service station, what actions will you take to get better business.

CHAPTER 8

Cases in International Marketing

Case Study - 1

MANOJ GOES INTERNATIONAL

Manoj Ranade visited China for the purchase of materials for doing interior decorations of his newly-built bungalow. While he was in China, he found that the textile industry offered the latest fashion garments at throwaway prices, delivered in India and the quality was reasonably good. They were willing to put labels as suggested by the customers and were also willing to give the packaging materials for the same.

After coming back to India, Manoj started surveying the market and he found the following-

1. There was no price control on fashion garments and the margins were very high.

2. Taxes were not high and the excise duty was applicable only for a textile industry having a large set-up. So most players had gone in for contract manufacture of textiles and its processing, thus avoiding excise duty.

3. Shopkeepers were not keeping proper books of purchases and sales and many times, purchased goods without proper invoice; avoiding sales tax (VAT).

4. Credits offered to shopkeepers was for long periods ranging from 90 to 180 days.

5. If credit was not offered, the shopkeepers refused to stock that particular brand.

6. Many major companies were going through franchisee outlets model to control credit periods and get visibility.

7. Duplicates of the brands were easily available as copyright protection agencies were not functioning. Many times it was difficult to distinguish between the copy and the original as the contract manufacturer sold the products directly to others.

8. Government offers reduction in VAT for ready-to-wear children's clothes, that is never passed on to the consumers. It becomes additional profit margin for them.

9. Most of the reputed brands were owned by the Aditya Birla group.

10. Customers liked to wear foreign sounding brands and did not like to purchase Indian brands.

11. Customers were willing to buy fashion garments with foreign sounding names at any price,

especially if they were well-advertised using celebrities.

12. Textiles purchased in bulk were available at a throwaway price and could be stitched locally also at a very low cost, using the mushrooming tailoring industry.

13. Wrinkle-free polyester blends and 100% cotton were more in demand.

14. As tailors were charging very high stitching charges and took longer time for delivery, more and more customers were opting for ready-mades.

15. Customers were willing to look alike and one could see 10 people wearing the same brand with the same colour and design.

Manoj, after finalizing the brand name and logo signed a contract with a local manufacturer and gave him a lot of a particular textile in various colours and ordered garments in the most saleable sizes of 'XS', 'S', 'M', 'L', 'XL' and 'XXL' in shirts, and trousers in the range 26 to 40 inches. Manoj ordered clothes and packaging materials from China also after sending them the brand labels, and started searching for franchisees.

Manoj appointed five franchisees to start with and gave them a fixed shop design to make them look identical. The franchisees paid deposit money and purchased all the stock with advanced money. This helped Manoj recover his entire investment and costs as he had purchased the textiles on long credit and the manufacturer was willing to wait for getting the next order. Manoj had to pay in advance to the Chinese suppliers and the transporters. Manoj went in for advertisements in glossy magazines and conducted opening ceremonies of the shops by celebrities.

Manoj is now a successful importer and manufacturer of ready-made garments and wants to expand beyond his initial five franchisees.

Questions

1. What challenges will Manoj face if he decides to import and sell ready-to-wear men's fashion wear?

2. What marketing strategy do you suggest to him for success?

Case Study - 2

I WANT TO BE AN EXPORTER

Rajaram was the son of a farmer producing various fruits like mangoes, papaya, pomegranates, grapes and a small quantity of paddy and beans. After completing his degree in agriculture he decided to join his father in farming. He wanted to be a successful farmer and did not want to be a run-of-a-mill farmer depending on Government support and loan waivers. He had studied agriculture and new technology and wanted to use it for his own benefit and better lifestyle. So he started studying the economy of producing fruits. He found the following facts-

1. All the farmers sold their fruits to agents at whatever rate they could get. Agents normally gave half the auction price declared in the trade papers. This barely covered the production cost, sometimes there was even a loss.

2. Taking small loads of fruits to the nearest city was uneconomical unless you sold the entire lot directly to the consumers at the prevailing retail rates (cost of transportation was high).

3. If you fought with the agent he would stop purchasing your yield, leading to total loss.

4. There was no storage facility to economically store the yield and then transport it in quantity.

5. If the yield was high the rates fell leading to loss, so it was better if yield was low and rates high.

6. Fruit pulp processing facility was available.

Rajaram found that the prospect of earning a good amount through farming was bleak and understood why many of his friends went to cities in search of jobs and were not interested in farming. On top of it, labour shortage was a major problem. The Government scheme of MGNREGA gave minimum 100 days rural employment at high rates, discouraging labourers to seek employment with other farmers. Rajaram was not going to get discouraged easily. He had heard of high rates if he exported his produce. He started checking up on it. He found that the rates were really high but the procedures were cumbersome and a lot of paperwork was involved. He checked the procedures for mangoes, bananas and pomegranates and they were the following-

1. Every country had its own list of rules and regulations.

2. Europe and America were strict about eradication of all possible germs and viruses from food.

3. Europe and America were strict about residual insecticides on all fruits and vegetables.

4. Most of the countries had their own packaging and label design regulations.

5. Products could be sold only to the importing agents in that country having a valid registration for importing.

6. There was a strict inspection of all the food products on arrival at these countries.

7. There was always a chance of the consignment getting rejected for one or the other reason.

8. Use of CFAs was required for ensuring that the cargo left the country in time by air and ensuring that all the paperwork was correct and complete.

9. Use of an exporting agent was advisable as he knew all the rules and regulations of most of the countries.

10. Use of exporting agents reduced the profits but ensured that there was no loss.

One more problem that came to light was that the export assistance in packaging was available for grapes and bananas in high export zones like Nasik and Jalgaon. For other fruits, it was either not available or was at Mumbai. Export agents insisted on some minimum quantity levels or else they did not accept the consignment or paid less.

Rajaram was bent on earning a good amount of money through farming and now he believed that export was the only way to earn good money. To ensure a minimum quantity of consignment, he decided to contact other farmers. He told them about the quality of fruits that could be exported and regulations on usage of insecticides and certain chemical fertilizers that were banned and the good rate that could be earned. Not many farmers showed interest in exports. Some asked him to buy from them at the prevailing market rates and do whatever he wanted to do. Rajaram decided to go ahead with the arrangements and along with that, persuaded some farmers to give him their land on lease, where he could grow fruits for export. He was able to get a large amount of land adjacent to his farm from this arrangement.

All the while, all his friends and family members asked him to forget about the export business and do what all the others did. But Rajaram always wanted to become an exporter. In the course of a few years, he started exporting all his fruits and started earning a good amount of profit.

Questions

1. Do you think Government is creating enough facilities to help exporters of agro products? Give reasons for your answer.

2. Are we blocking entry of dangerous products in our country? Give reasons to your answer.

3. What should be ideal system that will help increase exports of agro products.

Case Study - 3

EXPORT OF TOWELS

Paresh Kothari was studying in the second year of his MBA course when he was asked to do a project in entrepreneurship development. Being from Solapur, he found it easy to do a project in towel manufacturing. While working on the project he found that some of the manufacturers were manufacturing towels for export purpose, and these orders would be given priority as they were required to be completed in the given time. The earnings were much better and immediate (sometimes in advance) as compared to manufacturing towels for Indian markets. These orders were given to only a few towel manufacturers who had newer machines that were capable of manufacturing larger towels.

For submitting the project, Paresh and his team were required to make a complete project report that included-

1. Land requirement and cost.
2. Construction of shed for manufacturing office space and inward and outward storage of materials.
3. Permissions and licenses.
4. Manpower requirement and their wages.
5. Marketing requirement and costing.
6. Finance requirement and source and cost of finance.
7. Expected BEP (break even point).
8. Investment turnaround period.

The project report was required to be presented to the entire class and the students and the teachers could raise questions. Fifty percent marks were for presentation and question and answers. Paresh decided to become an entrepreneur after completing his MBA and start his own export-oriented towel manufacturing unit. Export orders were not regular and the exporters negotiated the rates very hard. Paresh decided to ensure that he set up his own export house also, so that he was not dependent on orders from other exporters. This way he could quote prices competitively and procure more orders. Paresh talked to his marketing professors about additional knowledge of export procedures than what was available in the curriculum. On their advice, he did an export-import course at the World Trade Centre in Mumbai. This helped him in two ways-he got introduced to exporters, Government officials in the Export Promotion Department (who came as faculty) and employees of some export houses (who were students). With all these contacts he could join an export house after the completion of his course.

While doing apprenticeship with an export house he learned many tricks of the trade, including the methods of sending pro-forma invoices, choice of country for export, foreign currency transactions, export packaging, insurance, quality certifications, payment terms, modes of payments etc. When Paresh felt that he could start on his own, he hired a small office space in Mumbai and started quoting for towels and bed sheets (Solapur variety). Because of his good contacts with the manufacturers, he could quote competitively and procure a few orders. After dispatching these orders, he wanted to set up his own unit. His father told him that there was one sick unit with good machinery which could be purchased at a much lesser price than actually setting up a new unit. The bank was ready to transfer the loans and all the permissions and licenses were valid. So Paresh would not be required to actually invest in high amounts. Paresh accepted his father's advice and went in for the purchase of the sick unit that could produce export quality towels.

sizingchart

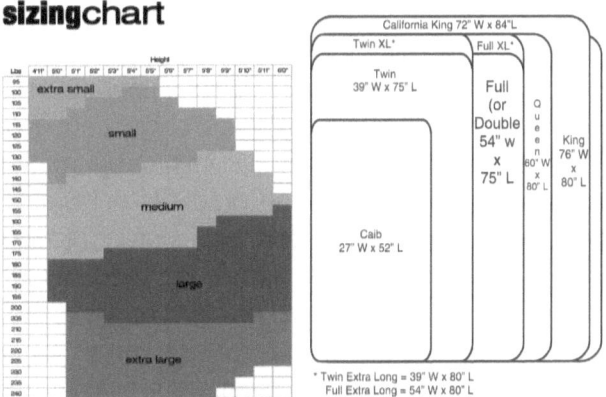

Fig. 8.1: Sizing Chart

For running the unit continuously at export quality production, Paresh contacted various malls who were willing to sell export quality towels. These mall owners said that they would sell the towels under their house brands. Paresh said that then they should purchase a minimum quantity decided every year and make him the monopoly supplier for at least five years. The mall owners accepted the terms and Paresh was assured his break even without any export order.

Paresh now controlled a major part of the towel export as he was giving the best quality at a short notice period. The other exporters also purchased bulk stock from Paresh and supplied to their clients.

Questions

1. What strategy did Paresh use to ensure that there was no failure in his business?
2. What suggestions would you give to Paresh for further exponential growth of his business?

Case Study - 4

DISTRIBUTION OF INTERNATIONAL PRODUCTS IN INDIA

Opening of international markets brought in a new opportunity for exporters as well as importers, more so for importers as exporters were subject to quality and standardization checks by the importing countries. But India was accepting all the products coming from Western countries as good and high quality products, without checking them at all. Since the products were coming in bulk and at a very low pricing, and Indian customers were willing to pay a high price for any imported product, it was a very prosperous business. Kirti Kotecha with his business of distribution in the western suburbs of Mumbai saw it as a good opportunity for business at high profits. Kirti Kotecha decided to go in for food products such as various sauces, tinned food and chocolates. He undertook a survey of the requirements and found that many of these products were wanted by many restaurants serving continental food preparations and importing in smaller quantity was found to be very expensive. The other lot was the international missions in India who needed these products for their employees and most of them depended on grey market imports in Crawford market shops, but many times these products were nearer to their date of expiry. Retailers in Crawford market were also willing to purchase these products, if available on a regular basis (off stock) and at a reasonable price.

Kirti Kotecha started negotiating with the suppliers in Europe and found that even after paying nearly 100% import duty and Mumbai city octroi, he was able to have the product prices below the locally manufactured MNC products. After adding the selling cost, the retailer margins and the VAT, the products could be sold at prices equal to locally manufactured products. The retailers were expected to sell these products at premium over locally manufactured MNC products getting high margins. If Kirti purchased a full container load, the prices went down further by another 25%. The food malls also showed interest in purchasing these products for attracting customers bent on buying imported products. Kirti decided to order smaller containers to begin with and see what happened before ordering bigger containers.

Kirti was able to liquidate the first container easily through his own distribution setup in the western suburbs, where many star rated hotels serving continental cuisine were present. In addition he sold some stocks to the Crawford market retailers and South Mumbai star rated hotels and restaurants serving continental cuisine. All of them were interested in purchasing the products on a regular basis and selling with high profits. Though the suppliers insisted on purchase of another container immediately, Kirti waited for a fortnight before he got an enquiry from the hotels again for more stocks. The delivery time was three weeks from the time the order was placed in normal conditions and could take around five weeks if loading in ships took longer time, due to non-availability of space. Kirti opted for Sri Lanka Shipping Lines as their rates were the lowest in safe passage categories (insurance companies declined to insure goods in other cheaper shipping lines for reasons of safety). Kirti wanted to avoid the glut in the market of these products, reducing the demand and so the price. He decided to order a smaller container every month so that he could keep the market demand up and prices high.

After three months, three small containers were sold and Kirti was making a good amount of money and had started getting orders from star rated hotels located in neighbouring cities like Pune, Nasik, Aurangabad, Vadodara and Ahmedabad. He also got trade enquiries from wholesale traders in other parts of India like Hyderabad and Bengaluru and so he had decided to order a full container this time and wanted to re-negotiate the rates for getting further discounts and/or longer credit period. On one such day, an officer from the Weights and Measures Department came looking for Kirti and said, "You are selling all these products in violation of the State Government rules and regulations." Kirti said that he had taken the import licence and was paying all the taxes properly and in time. The officer said, "Your products are violating the Packaged Commodity Act that requires-

1. Date of manufacture
2. Best before date (date of expiry)
3. MRP (maximum retail price)
4. Contact address in case of product complaint
5. Name and address of distribution agency in India
6. Multiple packages of products must be in multiple sizes and of the smallest/high selling pack e.g. 50 gm. 100 gm. 200 gm. etc. so that the customer can compare the prices.

Kirti managed to convince the officer that he was unaware of these rules and that he did not have any stocks but from the next lot onwards he would ensure that rules and regulations were followed. The officer demanded a monthly payout to look the other way as it was not noticeable whether the stock was imported and sold or was from the grey market. Kirti told him that he was not interested in doing business illegally and would adhere to rules from the next lot. The officer went back after taking money for the stock already sold in the market, since Kirti told him that he had imported only once and for a small quantity he could convince the officer to take a small amount.

Kirti talked to a printer and asked him to give a quote for stickers with all the information that could be pasted on all the products before they were sold locally. He also checked the number of stickers a person could stick in a working day and the cost of pasting per sticker. When Kirti talked to the suppliers he told them about the local Government stipulations and asked them to print the requirements. The suppliers agreed to print the date of manufacture and the 'Best before' date but refused to put the other information. Kirti asked them to give additional discount for getting the stickers printed and pasted, which they accepted.

Kirti now had a bigger responsibility viz to find out the MOP (market operating prices) of the product he was selling. The prices should not be lower than the price at which a majority of the retailers sold the products. He found that the retail margin earned by the retailers was almost 70-80% as the customers did not think twice before they purchased an imported product. The customer mind set was that the imported products must demand double the price of a locally manufactured product even if the quality of a locally manufactured product was much better. Kirti found that many local manufacturers were packaging their chocolates in international quality packaging and printing information in English and Arabic with barcode pricing to give it an imported look. These manufacturers did not print any local address and place of manufacture and sold the products at a good rate and retailers kept selling these products, as imported products from the grey market. This helped everyone to make money at the cost of gullible customers willing to pay a high amount for imported products.

Kirti checked the regulations on printing of MRP as compared to manufacturing or selling price. There are no regulations on it, at all and many manufacturers of various products kept high retail and wholesale margins on their products (e.g. kitchen utensils having MRP Rs.350/- were available for example at say Rs.100/- in wholesale, for the door-to-door sales people). He was happy to know that he could print the highest price at which the products were being retailed. Kirti decided to put the MRP in barcode instead of numerical on the packs and in numerical on the outer packing. This way he was safe on the rules and regulation front.

Kirti is well-settled in the business and has taken more imported products for distribution.

Questions

1. What are the requirements of starting an import business?

2. What strategy did Kirti adapt to ensure steady orders from the retailers?

3. What suggestion would you give as compulsory regulations on imported products?

CHAPTER 9

Cases in
Strategic Marketing

Case Study - 1

ISMAIL SHAIKH'S BAKERY

Ismail Shaikh, a bakery owner was famous in his city for the best bakery products like sandwich bread, ladipav, patties, cookies, nankhatai and khari. After his son Amjad passed out of the Catering Technology Institute, he had started selling pizza bases successfully and had opened branches of his bakery all over the city through franchisee arrangements. Though his business had gone up after his son joined, the profit margins had become thin. Amjad wanted to start VALUE ADDED products like pizza and sandwiches at all the branches with coffee counters and turn all the branches into cafes. Ismail was sceptical about the idea as it needed investments and he feared that it might lead to losses as these products were being sold by international chains. He asked Amjad what made him think his idea would lead to success and his answers were-

1. International pizza chains sold the smallest pizza for Rs.60/-(vegetarian) and Rs.90/- (non-vegetarian). With very little toppings it could actually be sold for Rs.20/- and Rs.25/- respectively and could be home-delivered at an additional charge of Rs.10/- per pizza.

2. Sandwiches were being sold at Rs.40/-(vegetarian) and Rs.60/- (non-vegetarian) which could also be sold at much lower rates of Rs.20/- and Rs.30/- respectively.

3. Coffee was being sold at Rs.90/- which could be sold at Rs.40/-.

So if the store competed with the price range and quality it had a 100% chance of success. Since he was not planning for going all-India there was no promotional expenditure to be spent on ads on the TV and newspapers.

Questions

1. Do you agree with Amjad's theory? Give reasons for accepting or not accepting his views.

Case Study - 2

BLUE BIRD SPIRITS AND WINES

Blue Bird Spirits and Wines is an organization selling wines, and IMFL (Indian made foreign liquors) like Rum, Brandy and Whisky in all the segments like Normal, Deluxe, Premium and Super Premium segments. Lately the company found that their competitors were sponsoring sports events and other events like Film and TV Awards using their surrogate products for advertising. These surrogate products existed only in advertisements and not in actual shops.

The management decided to come out with an actual product that could be advertised regularly and which the customers could get acquainted with and would like. The success of the product could lead to regular advertisements at much lower costs and help establish the wines and IMFL brands in all the corners of the country. Marketing research suggested non-alcoholic energy drinks that could be sold in attractive cans to attract the young generation. Blue Bird decided to launch an energy drink that would vitalize consumer spirits in two minutes. The product would be available in 200ml cans and would be best sold in chilled conditions. Suggest

1. Market segmentation.
2. Distribution strategy.
3. Promotional policy for the same.

Case Study - 3

SUPER WHITE, THE MARKET LEADER

Mr. Sethi was going through the Economic Times reports on the sales of washing powders and found that though his company was the market leader by way of total sales in rupee value, it had lost its position of leadership in volume sales to another company that specialized in selling low quality washing powder at cheap rates. He ordered an immediate enquiry as to why this was not noticed by his marketing managers and why the products of this company 'Super White' were not visible in the market.

The results of the research were startling. Super White selected the rural market as their niche market and supplied the products in truckloads at very low rates and high margins to the distributors. Since Super White manufactured their products in the cottage industry sector with many sub-companies, they paid no excise duty and avoided paying sales tax also by supplying part of the consignment on cash transactions. The high margins helped the distributors to service the rural markets where the cost of distribution was very high.

Mr. Sethi started looking for options to counter this competition and regain the market leadership in rupee sales as well as volume sales. He had the following options-

1. To establish a subsidiary company and start manufacturing products in tax havens like Silvassa (UT) to reduce the tax burden.

2. Establish newer brands for rural markets that could be sold in rural markets at a competitive price with a higher quality.

3. Establish a rural marketing department that would sell all their products in the rural markets leading to the establishment of these products also in the rural markets.

4. Giving van working allowances to distributors if they worked in the rural markets.

Questions

1. What options will you suggest to Mr. Sethi? Give reasons for your choices.

C H A P T E R   10

Cases in Consumer Protection

Case Study - 1

THE COKE/ PEPSI PESTICIDE CASE

In the month of June2003, an organization declared that all the soft drinks in India contain higher pesticide contents than permitted levels in Europe. The organization declared their findings through the electronic and print media. There were many organizations asking the Government to ban these soft drinks as they were unfit for human consumption. The media was making all the noise and the soft drink companies came out with their own version and declared the soft drink safe and also said that the laboratory which came out with the adverse results was not having the latest equipment to check the pesticide levels, and that it was not a Government recognized laboratory.

The Government on their side, went on taking somersaults for once, declaring a ban, again cancelling and then again saying that they would ban once a competent authority certified the pesticide contents. Finally, the government set up a parliamentary committee to look into the matter and came up with suggestions in 6 months. The result was yet to be declared (though six months were over). Then it was decided that the results would not be declared as the parliament was getting dissolved in February 2004.

The sale of the soft drink dropped momentarily, to come up again and then the consumers had already forgotten the issue.

What do we get out of this case?

1. In India we do not have quality control laboratories which can give authentic results beyond doubt, or which cannot be contested/questioned by other authorities.

2. The soft drink companies declared that they got the quality control checked on a periodic basis, regularly from a world famous laboratory in Switzerland.

3. The water used by the soft drink companies was pesticide-free as pesticides were not found in the mineral water and the soda sold by them.

4. There were pesticide contents in the soft drink concentrate. The only chance of this was that of sugar syrup added using locally made sugar. The Government should check sugar for any pesticide residues. That however will not be done as it affects the vested interests of political parties (there already are reports that even milk sold has pesticide residues).

5. There is NO POLITICAL will to protect the consumer's interest. All the political parties took advantage of the situation and probably increased their election funds.

6. Public memory is short. The effect was momentary.

7. Consumer organizations in India are very weak. They cannot pressurize the Government to take rapid action in the interest of the consumers.

8. Many consumers thought that it was a political stunt to get election funds.

9. Many consumers felt that the stunt was to safeguard the interests of the sugarcane juice sellers who lost sales due to the launch of the soft drinks for Rs.5.

10. The net result was that the soft drink companies were doing roaring business without any additional quality checks from the law-enforcement authorities.

What should be the steps to prevent similar instances? For avoiding similar instances, the consumer organizations should force the government to start quality control laboratories in every district throughout the country. Currently these laboratories are available only in some states and many states do not have them, even in their capital cities. The Government quality checks must be made mandatory. The consumer organizations should become more aware and should not allow these matters to die down and allow the consumers to forget them.

Questions

1. How will consumer organizations help in avoiding such cases?

2. The quality testing laboratories must be set up in every district of every state in India, do you agree with the statement? Give reasons for your answer

3. Find how many quality laboratories for food testing are available in India currently. Do you think they are sufficient? Give reasons for your answer.

Case Study - 2

THE CASE OF TRANS RESORTS

Trans Resorts was a company incorporated in Chennai. The list of the directors showed a name called TN Sadashivan (said to be the brother of TN Sheshan, then the Election Commissioner). The company opened its office in Mumbai on Mint Road in a commercial building very close to the CS Terminus of the Railways. The office in Chennai was in T. Nagar. The company appointed agents to sell time-shares for the upcoming resorts in Ooty and Kodai. The resorts were of different types and the price range for the time-share started from Rs. 28,000 to Rs. 50,000 depending on the type.

As the resorts were not ready, the company promised to pay a rental to the members for not using it. Some few lucky ones were able to get the rentals for first year. The company put in conditions that every member must book the time-share well in advance to get it when they needed it.

After one year, the company changed its office in Chennai from T. Nagar to Annanagar. This was informed to all the members but the company failed to inform the change of address in Mumbai from Fort to Chembur. By the time people came to know the change of address, the office in Mumbai was closed and so also the Chennai office. The property in Ooty was disposed off, at very high capital gains and the owners disappeared.

A few members tried to track the people in Chennai. But the people in Chennai were not cooperative and if you did not speak the local language you could get no justice. The corrupt officials did not take any cognizance of the written complaints. A few members went to consumer organizations, but they declared an inability to help. The company must have made huge profits and the owners must be enjoying their life. What do we get out of this case?

In India there is NO control on the activities of the companies. Anyone can float a company and CHEAT people and vanish. The corrupt officers will take their share in the booty and suppress the matter.

Consumer organizations do not have TEETH to take action against such defaulters. There is no vigilance body to take cognizance of advertisements to lure consumers, and protect them. Similar companies keep coming and CHEAT consumers, but the media also is silent and does not give enough publicity to such things, to warn the consumers against getting cheated by them. The consumer organizations do not take cognizance of such things and wait for someone to make a complaint. By the time they take cognizance, people vanish with all the money collected. Can we not trace these culprits? YES we can, the law-enforcing authorities can. All the money is deposited in the banks. The account opening formalities can lead to the person who helped these companies open the account. The person who helped the company open the account, can lead to the people behind the crime. Also, the money from the company account is not withdrawn in cash. It is mostly transferred to other accounts. These accounts can lead to the culprits. Everything can be done but there has to be someone who follows the lead and does it. The law-enforcing agencies are highly corrupt and when questioned give answers like-

1. We have shortage of manpower.

2. We have shortage of funds.

3. We have too many cases and the other cases are more important than this case.

4. We do not get time to do our work, since we are always busy in security for the political leaders.

The only thing that can stop this is that the consumers should become more aware and should not allow themselves to get cheated.

Questions

1. What steps do you think that should be taken by Government to help consumers in getting their money back?

2. What preventive steps do you suggest to Government to stop such bogus/cheater companies?

Case Study - 3

SUPPLY OF MODERN BREAD TO PAUD ROAD AREA IN PUNE

The Modern Bread supplier in Paud Road area of Pune insisted on cash payments and was not very regular in his service. Because of this, most of the grocery and provision stores stocked bread from the rival brand which was a Pune-based company. This rival company distributor supplied bread to all the retailers on credit and supplied it twice a day. The retailers paid only for the stock which got sold. So practically there was ZERO investment and higher profit margin to retailers in selling the local brands.

Kothrud area is known for the residents who have shifted their base from Mumbai and its suburbs. These people had tasted the breads of such brands like Britannia, Wibs, and Modern etc. which are good quality breads. All these consumers were not happy buying the local brand.

When these consumers asked for the brand they wanted, they got the answer that there was no service of that brand in the area. So the choice was to buy the bread in Deccan area or buy the local brand. Some consumers purchased bread in Deccan and some purchased the local brand as they had no choice.

Mr. Vashishta was not a tolerant person and he insisted on buying Modern bread only. He would buy Modern or avoid eating the bread altogether. To make sure that the bread was available at the nearest store, he wrote a complaint letter to the Modern Bakery. Since the address was not available he wrote to the address printed on the cover of Modern Bread, that of the franchisee manufacturer. The letter took its own time reaching the company officials, who took cognizance of the complaint.

The following points were noted-

1. The distributor was located in the old city area.
2. The location of the distributor was far from Paud Road.
3. The sale was low as dealers asked for credit.
4. The distributor was not willing to give credit for Paud Road area.
5. The distributor visited the area once in two days.

To resolve the problem, the company officials took the following actions-

1. They appointed a distributor in Kothrud.
2. They insisted that he visit all the shops twice a day.
3. They asked him to give credit wherever possible and required.

This had the required effect and now Modern bread is available in all the shops in Paud Road area of Kothrud. If consumers are determined to get what they want, the shopkeepers cannot force them to buy an unwanted product. BUY WHAT YOU WANT.

Questions

1. Why do you think customers are not demanding quality products and quality service in India?
2. How can we change consumer mind set (Chaltahain attitude)?

Case Study - 4

MR. VASHISHTA GETS FRESH TEA EVERY MONTH

Mrs. Vashishta bought her grocery and provisions from the nearby stores. Mr. Vashishta always complained about the taste of the tea, and there used to be arguments between Mr. and Mrs. Vashishta over the taste of the tea. Mrs. Vashishta said that she was using the best of the brands but the taste and flavour was missing. They changed various brands but the problem persisted.

One day it so happened that Mr. Vashishta had a look at the tea packet. The packing date was 4 months old. Mr. Vashishta now knew the reason for the taste of the tea. He asked his wife to insist on a freshly dated tea pack. The retailer tried to convince her that the company supplied 2 to 3 month old stocks, so it was not possible to get fresh stock anywhere. Mr. Vashishta tried in the city's central area and at some renowned stores where he could get fresh tea packs. While buying tea, he also bought some other provisions, and that became a practice. Their earlier shopkeeper found that their purchases were reducing and he asked Mrs. Vashishta the reason which she explained.

From the next month onwards the shopkeeper started getting fresh stock of tea for Mr. Vashishta. It was revealed later that the shopkeeper was buying the provisions from the wholesale market instead of the company authorized distributors (the company authorized distributors asked for immediate payment or a post-dated cheque). The wholesalers always had old stock as they had purchased it in bulk for getting the benefit of quantity purchase schemes (QPS), and kept selling it till it lasted.

Do not believe on the shopkeeper ALWAYS, he is there to earn money and not for giving social service. He will do only what helps him earn MORE money. Insist on what you want and you will get it.

Questions

1. How can we make consumers aware of expiry dates on packaged commodity?

2. Why do you think consumers accept what is available at door step?

Case Study - 5

MARUTI DEALER'S SERVICE STATION

All the car manufacturers give the facility of three free services after the purchase of a car. All these three services are supposed to be completed within one year of purchase of the car. Mr. Vashishth was a diehard fan of Maruti cars as his first car was (given by his company) a Maruti van and the second (which he had purchased) was a second-hand Maruti 800. The third car he purchased was again a Maruti 800 but this time it was a brand new one from a reputed Maruti dealer. After using the car for three months, he gave the car for the first free service. At the time of giving his car for service he informed the supervisor that the bolt for the extra tyre was not fixed after attending to the flat tyre earlier and it was in the dickey and showed it to the supervisor.

Next day when he got the car back he was charged for fixing new clutch plates and also for the bolt of the extra tyre. Mr. Vashishth raised the point with the billing clerk but they insisted on the payment of the money. Mr. Vashishth paid the money but sent an e-mail to customer care on the Maruti website. He raised the point saying that the bolt was shown to the supervisor so how could the clutch plates be worn out within three months and that too for an experienced driver like him, who had never had to change clutch plates of his earlier vehicles for two years.

His e-mail was replied to immediately by the Customer Care Department and he received a call from the CR (Customer Relationship) Manager that he would like to meet him. When the CR Manager came he tried to convince Mr. Vashishth that the clutch plates were really worn out and he was willing to refund the amount of the bolt in the next bill. Mr. Vashishth insisted on complete refund immediately. The CR Manager said that he needed to talk to his higher-ups before he took any decision. Mr. Vashishth informed the Maruti customer care about the discussion.

Next day the CR Manager came to meet Mr. Vashishth with the refund cheque and a goodwill gift. The next free service was again due after another three months. The service station again charged for replacement of clutch plates and this time one music CD that had remained in the music system was stolen. Mr. Vashishth again made complaints to the Customer Care Department of Maruti along with the previous details. This time he wrote them about the third free service that was mandatory for getting warranty validated. He informed the company that he did not want the third service done by the dealer as his experience of the earlier two services was bad.

This time the CR Manager of the dealer came along with a refund for the entire bill amount (including oil change etc.) and apologized. He also brought a goodwill gift along with the refund. Mr. Vashishth got his third service from an authorized service station and has never gone back to the dealer. He also tells everyone not to purchase vehicles from the dealer.

Questions

1. Has the Customer Care Department done its job well?

2. What punishment would you suggest for the dealer?

Case Study - 6

SERVICE CONTRACTS OF SAFE KEEPERS LTD.

Safe Keepers Ltd. is a well-known company in India with diversifications into various businesses like

1. Almirahs, safes and locks.
2. Office furniture.
3. Refrigerators.
4. Washing machines.
5. Typewriters.
6. Photocopiers.
7. Soaps and detergents.
8. Room fresheners.
9. Insect repellents.
10. Cattle feed.
11. Poultry.
12. Real estate.

The company was started during the British Raj and after Independence, had grown multi fold, when the new generation started utilizing the vast tracks of land that were purchased by the owners which became priceless collections. While the business went on growing due to increase in the demand and higher and higher purchasing power and changes in lifestyle, the company lost market share to new entrants because they did not change their product-oriented marketing approach. They felt, "People seeking GOOD quality will always come to us." This was true initially but slowly new entrants, after gaining market share and being able to invest in technology overtook them in quality also and the company further lost their market share. Newer generations born after independence are not brand-loyal like the earlier generations and are willing to try newer brands and stick to the newer brands if they find them better.

The company never appointed dealerships for their engineering products like Almirahs, safes, locks, office furniture, refrigerators and washing machines and insisted on selling these products through their limited showrooms in major cities. This limited their after-sales service and customers were unhappy with it. Another disadvantage of this system was limited exposure to the brand, and non-willingness to market operating prices (MOP) of the products. Normally when a dealer orders a higher quantity of any product, he gets higher discounts and also bonus in cash and kind (dealers prefer bonus in kind like trips to foreign locations, as they are not accounted in their income anywhere, thus saving them taxes), if he achieves higher targets. These dealers offer higher discounts to customers to achieve higher turnover in a short duration (festival season) for competing with other brands (prices of all products are high at company showrooms and lower in dealer outlets). Most of the dealers get credit for payment of products (up to 60days) and if they sell the products within that period, they are making a profit without actually investing in those products, thus increasing their ROI. Since Safe Keepers only worked through company-operated or franchisee showrooms, these benefits were not available to them and so the growth was limited and slow.

Similar problems were faced by their FMCG and cattle feed divisions also. In FMCG, they went in for contract manufacturing of other brands in a big way and a situation arose when almost 60% of the soaps and detergents manufactured in India were manufactured at Safe Keepers' manufacturing facilities. In cattle feed, because of their patented and monopoly products, though their business was not growing, it was steady.

A new General Sales Manager in the engineering products division wanted to reduce the complaints about the after-sales service and introduced the appointment of franchisee service contractors. The scheme that was started for refrigerators and washing machines is as follows-

1. All the new customers purchasing refrigerators and washing machines would be entitled for free service contracts for three years.

2. After three years, the contractor was authorized to extend the service contracts through AMCs (annual maintenance contracts) signed by the customers.

3. To increase the base of the customers under AMCs, the franchisee could enroll old customers who were using the Safe Keepers' products purchased before this scheme had been launched. The franchisee would assess the condition of the refrigerators and if satisfied, would enter into an AMC.

4. The conditions in the AMC were as follows-

   • The service would not be charged.

   • The spare parts changed were chargeable.

   • The service engineer would make a quarterly visit to inspect the customers for preventive maintenance, if any.

- No visit fees were to be given for the service engineer and up to four visits a year afterwards, it was chargeable (Rs.150/- per visit).

5. The franchisee was authorized to have AMC camps at various housing societies, and they were provided with foldable stalls with banners of the company for the purpose.

6. The AMC would be done in the name of the Safe Keepers Company and not the franchisee. So the customer made payments to the Safe Keepers Company and not the franchisee.

The franchisee saw this as a good opportunity to collect a lot of money in the name of the company and they went all out to enroll maximum customers under the AMC and even offered early bird discounts. The modus operandi was simple- the franchisee representative would meet the housing society Chairman/Secretary and take permission for erecting the stall for two days and distribute leaflets in all the flats and houses nearby. He would visit the customer who showed interest and collect the payments and then go to other areas. The franchisee collected a lot of money but knew that he would be required to give proper service to lots of customers who were deprived of service for many years.

Mr. Vashishth was one such customer who enrolled for AMC. The AMC charges were Rs.1000/- with early bird discount of Rs.100/-.So he had paid Rs.900/- by account payee cheque in the name of Safe Keepers' Ltd. The service engineer visited Mr. Vashishth, inspected their 320litre double door refrigerator that was two years old and certified it to be in a good condition to enter AMC. After two months of entering the AMC, the refrigerator developed problems in the cooling system and needed servicing. The service engineer, for his convenience, took the refrigerator to his service station and after completing the service returned the refrigerator back to Mr. Vashishth and gave him a bill of Rs. 3500/- towards the service charges. The bill did not show any replacement of parts but only transport to and from the service station, visit fees and labour charges. Mr. Vashishth refused to pay, saying it was part of the AMC and he was not liable to pay anything. The service engineer threatened to take back the refrigerator and said that when Mr. Vashishth paid, he would be required to pay for one more trip of taking back the refrigerator and bringing it back. Mr. Vashishth paid the amount as the absence of the refrigerator was causing problems of storage of food. He then wrote to the Safe Keepers' company headquarters and demanded refund of the money. The letter was replied to by the regional sales and service office saying that the Area Manager would visit and sort out the matter.

When the Area Manager visited Mr. Vashishth, Mr. Vashishth questioned the demand of Rs. 3500/-.The Area Manager responded saying, "You have paid only Rs.900/-.How can you expect the company to spend so much?" Mr. Vashishth asked him, "Have you ever taken an insurance policy? If you get injured in an accident immediately after taking insurance, what compensation do you expect? Only the premium paid, or the entire insured amount?" The Area Sales Manager could not convince Mr. Vashishth and said, "If you want to opt out of AMC, I can arrange to pay back your Rs.900/- but nothing more."

Mr. Vashishth then wrote to the Managing Director of the company along with the entire correspondence. The MD's office replied, "We are asking the sales office to take appropriate action." The sales office sent a letter saying that they could refund his AMC amount but could not refund the bill amount. Mr. Vashishth then sent another letter to the MD's office saying that if his claim of Rs.3500 + Rs.900 (AMC) was not settled within one week, he would send the entire correspondence to the newspaper office along with the names of other unsatisfied customers. He would also lodge a complaint with the consumer court. This worked well and within 10 days, a draft of Rs.4400/- was received by Mr. Vashishth.

Today Mr. Vashishth advises all and sundry not to purchase any products of the Safe Keepers Ltd. or take them even if they are offering it at a very low cost.